ALSO BY ROBERT KIPNISS

Robert Kipniss: A Working Artist's Life
Robert Kipniss: Paintings and Poetry 1950-1964

SHINE

Robert Kipniss

Four Directions Press
Rhinebeck New York

Published in the United States by Four Directions Press,
P. O. Box 417, Rhinebeck, New York, 12572.
www.fourdirectionspress.com

ISBN 978-0-9981144-4-6

LIBRARY OF CONGRESS CONTROL NUMBER 2017959502

Printed by CreateSpace, an Amazon.com Company

Published November 2017
FIRST EDITION

Available from Amazon.com and other book stores
Book and cover design by Sean McCarthy

To Corona, 1942-1944

CHAPTER ONE

GIOVANNI MADE SURE his son understood the great danger if anyone learned he didn't go to school. The boy adored his father and knew quite well the wisdom of these repeated warnings: even at the age of eleven, he had a precocious instinct for the logic of cause and effect. There was an underlying sadness in their lives since the death of his mother more than two years before, and in their increased poverty they had moved into a place that was barely habitable.

"They won't get you, Americo. I won't let the system take you!" He looked lovingly at the boy as he assured him, "I will see you learn what you need. You will grow to be a man. You will know plenty enough for a good life." The son smiled and felt cared for.

"I will teach you honor, and to respect what you know is right. You will read everything, you will love learning."

Because for the most part of every weekday the young boy must never be observed by neighbors, weekday mornings he would sit reading. During the months that public schools were open, every week, Monday through Friday, he sat at their one table, in their one room; from eight in the morning until it was time to stop for lunch, at twelve. After eating and cleaning their few dishes, his father would instruct him in simple arithmetic. While school was in session the father, Giovanni, would not allow any possibility for a chance observer to learn the boy was at home, and so during the morning reading hours, and the afternoon arithmetic hours, he was forbidden to leave the house. He also avoided being near their one window where he might be seen, no matter that their little shanty of a home was shielded from the street by a tall privet hedge. This was their routine since they moved here from another district, and he was no longer registered in a school where his absence would be noticed.

Sometimes before beginning their arithmetic lesson, as he put away their few lunch dishes, the father would reaffirm his devoted protection, "I won't let the system get you, Americo. No, not me! Don't you worry about that!" And he would defiantly shake a fist in the air, this small, slight man with a strong voice. "Remember, no matter what, you stay out of the system! No matter what!" He would usually pause, and then he would add softly, lovingly, "Listen to me, Americo."

When he said his son's name he stressed the third syllable with an affectionate emphasis, and rolled the 'r.' "Amerrreeco." And at these times, as his voice lowered, his expression would grow troubled. "Just stay out of the system!" And with anger, mistrust and resentment he pointed a finger toward the window, indicating the menace of the world outside.

For more than two years now, his father remained partially crippled from an accident at his former job. Using a cane he could get around a little, but not well enough to be employed. Each month a small check came in the mail, and together with what Americo could earn, (when school hours ended and it was safe for him to be seen outside) they were able to get by. They even saved a little.

His mother had died a few months before his father's accident, and the loss of her loving presence, as grievous as it was, was further intensified by the loss of income from her work as a cleaning-lady in a wealthy neighborhood. When that happened they moved near the marshy fringe of Corona, finding a barely standing one room home at an unusually low rent. It was 1943 and Corona was a poor Italian section of Queens. It wasn't a slum. The people there had pride, and the fronts of their houses and sidewalks were always kept neat and clean. Here, in this community of unusually meager resources, they, father and son, were among the poorest of the poor, at a time when there were plenty of poor neighborhoods.

Giovanni often said how lucky they were to have found this little hovel, helping the boy to feel his life was good. And, indeed, he felt fortunate in his father's love, protection and the occasional advice that seemed so much like the wisdom of a tribal elder. Their home was a structure made of three wooden walls with the outer side covered with imitation brick siding, and a tar-papered plywood roof covered with tin. The fourth wall was the exterior of the two story building to which this room was attached, built by the owner to get a little bit of extra rental income. It was equipped with only the meager essentials of subsistence. From the mother structure they received heat, electricity, and cold water. A vent brought in heat during the winter months, and plumbing was in the corner where there was a narrow closet housing a toilet. Outside the toilet door was a small sink below a narrow shelf that held a double-burner hot plate and an aluminum toaster which long ago had lost its shine. Next to that was a small bathing tub which could be filled to a shallow depth with a mixture of cold tap water and water boiled on the hot plate. When it wasn't in use it was covered by a thick wooden board painted with white enamel, serving as a broad counter when they prepared meals.

It may or may not have been certified legally habitable by the city; still, it was only fourteen dollars a month, and despite how primitive it was, this bare-bones situation was workable and appreciated. Giovanni knew that in the eyes of the system, which he perceived as nothing more than a heartless, numbing grind of bureaucracy, this home was woefully substandard for raising an eleven year old child. Should their situation become known Americo would certainly be taken from him and placed in one of the county's "homes." The law didn't allow for distinctions between cases, and in the guise of being concerned it often seemed the state punished children found living outside its methodical definitions. As if what they would give him would be acceptable! Giovanni would tell the world: nothing could be better for his son than to remain with him, to be taught and loved, and to be so deeply cared for, that is, if only it were safe to say anything.

CHAPTER TWO

GIOVANNI HAD SOME small skills. One afternoon his landlord allowed him the use of a few tools, and, with scraps of lumber found in a vacant lot, he built a nicely designed shoe-shine box for his son. With an old belt attached as a strap it could conveniently be carried over one shoulder. For less than a dollar he bought shoe polish, a tin of black and a tin of brown, a brush and a buffing cloth. By adding two rags for applying the black and the brown, he had created a reasonably well-outfitted business for his son. Later, from a street-corner trash basket, he salvaged a small, flat, leather pillow filled with horse-hair. Folded in half it fit easily under the hinged top of the shine-box, and the boy used it to kneel on while he worked.

At three o'clock on week-days Americo received two nickels from his father, picked up his shine-box, walked over to One Hundred and Eighth Street, and for one of the nickels

11

took the bus to Forest Hills. The other nickel was for his return fare in the event of an emergency, or if for some unusual happenstance he earned no money. He rode to the intersection where One Hundred and Eighth Street crossed Queens Boulevard and became Continental Avenue.

"I'm off, poppa." Americo kissed his father's cheek. Ten after three. It was safe.

"Good luck today." The father patted his son's mop of curly dark hair, and kissed his forehead. "I'm always proud of you." Americo knew how deeply he meant what he said.

In those years, the early 1940s, Forest Hills and Corona were separated by a large area of what seemed to him a foreboding marsh, or, what we would call today, a small wetland, (now long ago filled in and built up with acres of tall, brick apartment buildings). When passing the edge of the Corona side he held his breath to keep from gagging. The marsh was divided by Horace Harding Boulevard, and the Corona side had perpetually bad odors, its far end sporadically used as a place to dump garbage, at night, by individuals from slightly better neighborhoods.

For this young boy, crossing into Forest Hills was much like entering another country. The air smelled strangely pleasant and clear in a way that had him feeling unsure he was dressed well enough, or that his person was bathed recently enough. Here people dressed differently from the ways with which he was familiar; their clothes were clean and freshly pressed, without wrinkles or worn edges, and with no tell-tale signs of repaired hand-me-downs. Everyone seemed to stand easier, not bent with the cares and calamities of basic survival. It was curious to him that their skin seemed pinker, and their grooming so much more noticeably looked after. And when these people walked in the streets they didn't look at each other. There were no greetings, no friendly nods, no acknowledgment that they weren't alone. Until these trips he had never considered that there might be significance in the outward appearance of the people in his neighborhood. Now he felt he lived in another world, and pondered the differences between these two neighboring communities. Immediately he knew one thing: this would be a good place to make money shining shoes.

After a few weeks he became known as a good shine boy: instinctively he adopted an acquiescent manner, had little to say, and was diligent in his work. Surprisingly, most of his patrons were fifteen and sixteen year old sons of what he reasoned must be very wealthy families, and he inwardly marveled that it seemed so natural for them to enjoy posturing with one foot up on Americo's shine-box, puffing on cigarettes, lords of this little corner. It had become local custom that after school and in the evenings this corner was theirs, in front of a large Rexall Drugstore, near a newsstand and a set of stairs to the subway. They chatted and joked, smirked at passing girls and young women, and made attempts at suave innuendo, imitating smart phrases from current movie dialogue.

Americo didn't have much to say, thinking mainly of the money he would earn, working for dimes, and the occasional sport who would make a little grand show of giving him a quarter.

"Here, boy. Shine!" And he would take his box over to the waiting customer. Some evenings he would try to establish a place for himself closer to the subway exit and get more adult customers on their way home from work, returning from what

13

he imagined to be the magical big city. He had never been there, but once in a while his father took him to the movies, and when the drama took place in New York City, and there were scenes of some of the grander landmarks, his father whispered explanations in the darkness. Going to the movies was a big treat after a stretch of gray weather and too many days of cold, sunless monotony. And in the smaller, local theaters there usually would be a double feature, plus a short Pathé News, mostly of the frightening war, which we were not yet winning, and a cartoon. It puzzled the boy to see footage of the terrible war and then a cartoon, usually of animated animals as human-like creatures tricking and hurting each other. Not finding them funny, he didn't laugh at these antics; in fact, he rarely laughed at all. He was not sad or depressed, just serious and prompted by a driving curiosity. It seemed odd that the audience surrounding him laughed and giggled. Humor wasn't part of his life.

The street traffic had an increasing number of sailors and soldiers on leave. They were always good for a quarter, when they wanted a shine, but in the discipline of army and navy life they pretty much always had nicely shined shoes.

"Hey, shine-boy, over here!" He liked that, and he liked being quiet. He heard his customer's conversations, and, while he didn't understand everything, it was nice to be listening because he had no friends, no exposure to the world that certainly would have put him away someplace if the wrong person ever learned about his life. And so he found working to be good, and he looked forward to it each day, in warm weather sweating too much, in colder weather glad to be moving vigorously.

When the weather was either rainy or too cold for the

teen-age crowd to congregate on "their" corner, or for anyone else to stop and stand for a shoe-shine, he went around the next corner to Austin Street where an old Italian gentleman ran a five chair barber shop. The elderly man recognized this well-mannered, dark-haired youngster as a kinsman and that he was in need, and allowed him to come in and shine the shoes of those customers who indicated their willingness.

"Hello, Americo. Nasty weather today, eh?"

"Hello, Mr. Battaglia. I can't make no money out there in that mess. Can I work here?"

He always asked, even knowing the answer.

"Sure, sure. Come in, get warm, make some money." He liked the young boy.

Mr. Battaglia was not one of those talkative barbers, nor were the other barbers he employed. His customers came in and he wordlessly showed them where to sit. Pretty much the only sound was the snipping of the scissors, which Americo found a pleasant counter-point to the rhythm of his polishing.

Sometimes when the barber closed shop at six thirty the boy went to the local bars where the clientele found his presence amusing as well as convenient. Once in a while a tipsy sailor would give him a whole dollar. But he preferred working outdoors, on the street corner, among the teen-aged boys who seemed so exotic.

Around five thirty he ate quickly the sandwich he brought with him; at eight-thirty it was time to take a bus home. Giovanni would smile with pleasure when his son put his earnings on their table. He sometimes said, "The world," gesturing toward the outside of their shelter, "they see you as a boy, but here," and he would pause for emphasis, "we know you are a man."

Chapter Three

"I ONLY HAD three years high school, but you need more. I know that, and you must know that too. You need to read, everything." He made sure Americo understood it was not only important to read but that he should discover the great pleasure in learning new things, and that if he found this pleasure he would develop a deep appreciation of the reading experience. As much as Americo looked forward to each new book there was also always a book for his father, his fellow student. The two of them would sit and read, the son to learn of the world, and the father, in his enforced idleness, hoping to find in books an idea of something worthwhile he could do, even in his crippled state. As they read, each engrossed in very different intellectual worlds, they were aware of a deep togetherness.

The father would write down titles and authors remembered from his own school days, and at the library Americo took out books for the two of them. History, novels, geography, Americo enjoyed reading everything. And he quickly learned that by reading the introductions in the front of the books there would often be mention of related books, either to enumerate additional and perhaps lesser known titles by that same writer or to introduce the work of other authors, to form a comparison. Sometimes he would want to read more by a certain author, or read about his or her life, and his father would encourage him to follow his desire. Sometimes he would stop reading without even realizing it, and sit and daydream. At such times his father would smile, and be careful not to disturb him, knowing the value of dreams.

Giovanni had developed an understandably necessary attitude of mild paranoia.

"You didn't talk too much, did you?" He would ask the boy upon his return from the library, or the grocery store, or any place he had been.

"Don't say too much! Do what you have to do and say good-bye. Be friendly, be polite, but no conversation. You know, talking leads to talking, and then the questions. Always the questions!"

"I know, poppa. You told me, you know you told me. You tell me this every day."

"Yes, yes, but I have to be sure. Because after the questions comes the system! I keep you out of the system! I do this. Me. You listen to me."

"Yes, poppa! You know I listen."

In matters of importance Giovanni tended to be repetitive

because he understood the finality of mistakes.

At three o'clock it was the end of the outside world's school day, and safe for the boy to emerge from their little home. Sometimes children were playing on the street, younger, but not older. By the age of twelve most of the young people found some kind of after-school employment: sweeping a store, a sidewalk, delivering groceries. There was always work one could do to make some bit of income. It had to be a very marginal job because the legal working age was sixteen.

Among his library visits Americo met a girl. He had seen her before, both on the street and in the library, and they had exchanged hellos. They talked a bit about the book she was reading. They whispered softly, to avoid disturbing the three or four readers, older men and women who were usually there, at the tables. Annette told him the book was for reading on the subway, and she was hurrying to join her father at his corner in the city, where she helped him sell newspapers. She explained the evening rush hour started at five and she needed to be there early to help set up the large bundles of late afternoon editions. (In those days newspapers had three or four editions during each day and evening.) Her father's newsstand was made of a wide plank across two empty orange crates with piles of papers on top, the News and the Mirror, two cents each; the Times, the Post, the Tribune, and several others, all a nickel each.

"We got a good spot. By a big subway entrance!"

What the boys and girls in this neighborhood earned wasn't to have pocket change. Like Americo they, too, brought home their earnings and put them on the kitchen table, to be counted and added to their family's resources. The only days off were Sundays, when virtually all businesses stayed closed.

This was a family day: church, Sunday supper, then maybe a ballgame in the park, or a visit to relatives. For Americo it was a day to rest, read for an hour or two, and then take a nice long walk, exploring beyond the immediate neighborhood. Sometimes he would go as far as Elmhurst.

The depth of poverty in the area was not uncommon for those years, and a number of the homes were without indoor plumbing. In school the children, separated by gender, had a class period each week devoted to the luxury of taking showers, a necessary hygiene break that kept the students reasonably clean. Americo would learn these things from an infrequent conversation with one or another of the neighborhood kids, and for this, and the devoted protectiveness of his father, the daily pleasure of reading, and absolutely the adventure of going to work every day, he felt his life was good, and even somewhat privileged.

In his awareness of life he had no sense of deprivation. The pleasure in learning more and more about the world became deeply absorbing, leaving no room in his mind to think of being needy, of wanting more. And there were so many books in the library.

Before going to work he made himself a sandwich: two slices of salami, a slice of cheese, a little mustard. When he became surer of his business instead of packing his dinner he went to the local dime store's lunch counter. There he tried something as yet unknown to him and it quickly became his new favorite food: a large scoop of warm chop suey on a soft roll, for ten cents, and with a soda and five cents worth of pretzels, which he dipped in the mustard pot by each place setting, he could really dine, and still have change from a quarter. Not as economical as a sandwich from home, but he felt it was necessary, and that he could afford it. His father agreed, adding that he was a hard worker and deserved to enjoy food bought with money his labor earned. The boy preferred to avoid eating on the street while he was working, and this could be done in less than fifteen minutes, missing out on no more than one customer, if that.

The only thing he really didn't like was the very cold weather. He always combed his hair before going to work, and because he disliked his natural curls he would wet his thick mop of dark hair to comb it flat, even though it curled up again as it dried. When the temperature fell into the twenties, and lower, the water in his hair froze while he waited for the bus. Worse, while he rode in the warm bus the ice melted, and the cold drops ran down his neck, under his collar.

He liked riding on the bus. The trip took about twenty minutes, the seats were comfortable, and the passing streets entranced him. He was particularly intrigued by the several changes of architecture as he moved from the wooden two and three family houses on the gray streets in his neighborhood across the marsh to the many blocks with rows upon rows of neat, well-cared for modest two story attached houses in Annandale. He admired their clean cream-colored stucco exteriors with driveways that sloped downward under their first floors into one-car garages. From there the bus went on to the more sedate tree-lined streets in Forest Hills, where he was continually struck by how everything looked more tasteful as well as expensive beyond imagining. He wasn't just passing time as he went through his life; he looked carefully at what he saw. It was all so vivid and meaningful in ways he wasn't yet clearly sure about.

In their part of Corona he and his father lived in a neighborhood where people were warm although they minded their own business. There was a line between warm and too friendly, a line that was never crossed. What they noticed they noticed, but they didn't pry, and if among friends or acquaintances they talked about what they saw going on among one or another of their neighbors, it was always quietly and with discretion, without fuss, with no wish to humiliate or to cause trouble.

Giovanni and Americo had been there more than two years now, were of no bother to any one, and were accepted into the community even as they were pretty much left to themselves. They were greeted by name on the street, and welcomed in the small Italian delicatessen on their block, and in the larger grocery store two blocks away, both family owned businesses. On their local business street there was also a storefront bakery, which was never anything out of the ordinary except at Easter and Christmas when they went to decorative extremes with colorful, even gaudy, religious images on the cakes: lambs, crosses and flags, angels and Santas. There was also a shoe repair shop where much worn out footwear was given a year or two reprieve from the trash bin, and the public library. Without exception, in this neighborhood every place of business had a framed photo portrait of President Roosevelt on the wall behind the cash register, so commonplace that after a while you never noticed them.

The tenor of life in the street was busy with the business of every day's simple challenges. There was almost no crime and so there was little fear. Everyone knew there was a serious undercurrent of attention following the daily radio reports of the far-away war, and they trusted and prayed that our boys would be up to protecting the country.

Amid all this, Giovanni was only fearful of losing his son to the bureaucratic authorities, and he was ever vigilant. "If they get you they gobble you up! They don't even spit out your bones!"

Chapter Four

"You had another good day, Americo."

"Yes, poppa. It was good. I didn't have to wait much between shoes."

"Our savings are beginning to grow a bit. Look."

He lifted a ten inch piece of loose floorboard near one corner of their room and removed from underneath the floor a small tin box. He flipped the lid and took out a wad of bills. "We have over eighty dollars! Imagine!"

The boy was as proud of his father as the father was of his boy.

"And I still have my lucky two dollar bill. Everyone knows that's good luck."

"I don't think there are many of them."

"That's why they're good luck."

He smiled and continued, "I showed you before, but look

again. This one is special." Removing his right shoe he took from it a clear celluloid folder the size of a bill folded in thirds. He unfolded the bill. "The numbers are the same, backwards and forwards. See?

12577521. The boy looked and nodded, impressed with his father's observations.

Giovanni's only other possession of value was a ring he regarded as another good luck talisman, a diminutive gold pinky ring given him by his late wife early in their marriage. It had a Chinese character in raised relief which he had been told signified good luck, and inside the band was inscribed, "Amore, Philomena."

"Someday this will be yours, Rico." He didn't often use the boy's name in its diminutive. "It's all I have for you, but when someday it comes to you, it will be with great love."

Americo became uncomfortable when his father talked like this and, thankfully, it wasn't often.

Life in the neighborhood was without much room for frills or nonsense. Each day's struggles were elemental and basic. Yet there was no sense of despair or sadness. They had their families, which always came first, and their earnestness to deal with continuing needs. And they prayed for their men and boys in service, who were off in one or another of the armed forces. Here there was a simple awareness of how the elements of life were related. For most of the residents there wasn't much of a safety net: if they didn't work this week, the next week they didn't eat so good.

"Americo, let's go to the movies. What do you say?" It was late March, winter, in its dreariest month, was close to over, and spring was almost ready to show itself. Now when there was a breeze it had a softer edge, a gentleness, no longer raw and deeply chilling. There was an air of encouragement as the daylight noticeably began to linger later into the early evening.

"Sure, poppa. Nice."

Using a cane, and leaning slightly on his son, Giovanni could manage walking six or seven blocks. And every day, without assistance, he insisted on going out alone, for a half hour, to the grocery store for some shopping, to the deli to cash his check, or to buy another dried salami to replenish their larder, the shelf over their half-sized refrigerator.

CHAPTER FIVE

AFTER WALKING SLOWLY for about twenty minutes, as they neared Roosevelt Avenue, they passed a narrow alley between some one and two-story industrial buildings. In the shadows, about thirty feet into the alley, Giovanni saw a man lying on the ground next to a brick wall, and when he paused to peer at the sprawled figure he heard a groan.

"Americo! Look!" He helped his father hobble quickly to the fallen man. As Giovanni bent to look to see if the man on the ground was badly hurt another man appeared from the shadows behind them, and in a quick, practiced motion grabbed Giovanni's arms. At this the man lying on the ground leaped up and punched him in the face. When little Americo unhesitatingly lunged at the man restraining his father, kicking and punching him, the man let go of the father and delivered a sharp punch to the side of Americo's head, sending him to the ground, dazed. The father, his arms released, began beating at the other man with his heavy cane. Seeing this, the man who had punched the boy brought a knife from his pocket and stabbed the struggling father in the back. For a second or two Giovanni's entire body stiffened with the shock of this sudden, mortal strike. Then he fell to the ground, and while one thief took his wallet and loose change, the other, having seen the ring, spit on Giovanni's pinky and quickly worked the ring from it. Someone from somewhere near-by must have seen what was happening because as he took the ring there was the sound of a police siren off in the distance, and it was getting louder, closer.

Hearing the siren the man with the ring looked up, and in this movement his face entered a small patch of light coming between the buildings from a street lamp. Americo had begun to shake off his punch-dazed state, and shakily he got up from the ground. He looked at the assailant just as the man turned and looked at the boy, the man's features clearly discernible in that bit of light. For a moment the two intently looked at each other. The man started toward the boy but abruptly stopped as the noise of the siren took on urgency, getting louder and louder, and his partner began gesturing with sharp motions of agitation. He indicated to the other with a shrug of his head a direction in which to go, and they started running deeper into the alley, disappearing into the shadows, their footsteps quickly fading.

Americo rushed to his father, knelt, and grasped the man's shoulders, saying softly, over and over, "Poppa. Poppa. Oh, Poppa."

Giovanni's eyes opened. He looked at his son with his

last glimmer of life. And he heard the siren, now very close.

"Go home, Rico." His voice was weak. "Go home. Don't let the system get you." His voice was barely a whisper. "Stay out of the system, Rico." And he died.

Americo kissed his father on the forehead, and stayed still for a moment. With the sirens so close the police had to be just about to enter this alley. He rose up and swiftly ran through a narrow opening between the buildings, then through an empty lot, after which he slowed to a walk to avoid attracting attention. He tried to think but the best he could do was replay the awful event in his mind, to somehow absorb this deep loss, and to grasp the extreme peril of his predicament. The few blocks to his home took nearly an hour as he criss-crossed back and forth through the streets of his neighborhood, his mind a jumble of urgency, mourning and apprehension. He was too focused on surviving this calamity to allow the fear and grief he felt to completely take over his thoughts, and he tried to push the sadness from his mind as best he could, already aware he needed to understand how to manage his way through this sudden loss of the protection and wisdom of his father.

Eventually he allowed himself to come to the little dirt path that led, through a small opening in the tall privet hedge, from the street to the entrance of his shanty. With shaking hands he opened the lock and entered, closed the door, and in the dark room knew where to reach to turn on the lamp. But with the light on, this little room, his home, now seemed terribly unfamiliar, and appeared unexplainably large in its emptiness. How strange and different the world can seem with the addition or subtraction of only one person.

Alone in this room he was achingly aware of just how

alone he was in the world. There was no one to talk to, or to teach him, or to tell him what needed to be done. There was no one concerned about what would happen to him. And there was no one to love except in his memory. He was stunned by the silence, the stillness, his mind returning again and again to his new awareness that without his father, in this whole world there was utter disregard for his existence. He kept replaying the vivid pictures in his mind of the sudden, violent horror that would change his perception of everything, so surely changing his entire knowledge of existence, yet not able to understand it was only his own young life that was thrust into this isolation, an isolation that transformed his happy, vibrant earth into a derelict planet, lonely, empty, cold. He brushed his teeth.

After drying his face and his hands he sat at the table for a minute or two. Unsure of what to do, he stood up and walked around. There were two steel folding cots with thin mattresses which were folded up each morning and put against the wall. And there were two sturdy wooden chairs with a cushion on each seat. The chair that Americo's father sat in was an armchair. He put the kettle on the hot plate to boil water for tea, and when the water boiled he put in a twice used tea bag, added milk and six lumps of sugar, and sat in the armchair.

When he finished the sweet tea he washed his cup; there were no saucers. Then he got the dust cloth from the utility drawer in the kitchen cabinet, and carefully dusted the furniture. First the table, then the chairs and the night stand, which served as a lamp table, and the two lamps; the second was a standing lamp near the table at which they ate and read. Then he took the broom and swept the floor, carefully, even though he had just as carefully swept the floor before leaving for the movie house. Now his father was dead; a good man's life extinguished in a terrifying moment. He opened one of the cots, took off his clothes, turned out the light, and went to sleep. He was exhausted.

His sleep was dreamless, or if there were dreams he did not remember. When he awoke in the morning it was a moment or two before he re-entered his new reality, and as he digested what he could manage to think about, there was a devastating pain of emptiness in the core of his body. He decided it was of the most importance that he try to think through, as logically as he could, what he must do, and what he must not. And that it would be better to do nothing than to do the wrong thing. He ached for the loss of his father.

CHAPTER SIX

WHEN HIS MOTHER died he was bereft and nearly desolate, but his father was there to comfort him, and they grieved together. And while not for a moment did they neglect their grief, with his father's willful strength they were able to move on with the physical necessities of daily life. Americo remembered this very clearly, and he used that memory as a plan for his survival. He would try not to let himself fall apart from grief or sadness.

But he was only eleven years old, and he felt terrible and sad.

Survival: his father's message as if dictated from another world to beware being "gobbled up by the system that wouldn't even spit his bones out!" As achingly as he felt the sudden lurid nature of this deepest of losses, he attempted to balance his grief by instructing himself to keep thinking of the very real monster that lurked just outside the walls of his home.

Suffering and practicality: strange bedfellows. The boy, mindful of his loss and the changes in every fiber of his grasp of the world, immersed himself as best he could in the mechanics of everyday life. In the morning he rose and folded the bed away, washed his hands and face, and made breakfast. Breakfast was always the same, toast with jam, hot tea with milk and sugar. He read until noon and stopped for lunch. He was using the armchair exclusively now, and in it he felt closeness with his father's spirit. And sitting in it he didn't have to see, in an unexpected glance, that it was empty

That the murder would never bring the police to his door was a certainty. With his father's wallet being taken there was no further identification in his pockets. The boy knew enough about police work from his reading, and the movies he had seen, to realize there were no records of his father's fingerprints since he had never been arrested for anything, ever. No, he, Americo, wasn't even a passing thought in police-think, and he would keep it that way.

Noticing he was almost finished with the books he had from the library, he had to plan another trip there, two blocks away. This was not only to return his books and get new ones but also to return his father's books, being sure to take out new ones for him, too, lest not doing so would stir suspicion. He checked the food supplies and made a short list of things to get at the grocer's and at the delicatessen. Within his intelligence there was as well a developing intuition, and he very clearly knew it would not be safe for him to go out with an expression that revealed his preoccupation with loss and shock, a look that would prompt pointed questions. Before visiting the local merchants who were so familiar with his usual sunny demeanor, he tried to think of things that were enjoyable and fulfilling. This was difficult but he devised a formula to succeed in this by thinking of certain memorably witty and upbeat passages he remembered from among the many books he had read, and he would replay them in his mind like a story on the radio each time he prepared to go out. Still, from eight in the morning until three in the afternoon, no matter what was needed, he would not leave his home, or go near the window.

Chapter Seven

Giovanni had reminded him, as a matter of daily routine, to practice a kind of paranoid carefulness of conversation with everyone, no matter where he was. Alone he was able to do this for a while, but he was alone too much and there was no part of his life where there were any personal words with another being. Gradually, ever so slowly, without Giovanni's constant reminders, his naturally pleasant disposition began to emerge. That, and the imperative of navigating through the many responsibilities of being completely self-sufficient, prevented him from retreating into self-pity. Grief he knew, and sadness, too, and this was most in his heart when he was alone in his room, in his father's armchair. Thankfully, his most constantly returning thought was of survival, and this pragmatic urgency kept him from being consumed by his sadness, and the tragic turn of his life.

In the midst of his awareness of painful loss he also found within himself a capacity for a zestful pleasure in just the most basic sense of being alive. Without being able to put these thoughts into words, he wanted to explore the world of feelings and relationships, to eventually grow into manhood and discover for himself all the intricacies he observed in the lives of the adults he met, both in his ordinary daily pursuits and of those he encountered in his wide and varied reading. Where Giovanni's wariness kept him turned inward, mostly in a one room life that was almost a jail, Americo's unfettered and insouciant curiosity led him, albeit still intelligently cautious, into the world. He knew great sadness but not depression.

Along with his intense emotional life his mind was acutely reasonable. Cause and effect were quite obvious and elemental to him. Certain things needed to be attended to or other things would go badly. It seemed simple, and he was far from being overwhelmed. To the contrary, he not only was well up to the challenge, the challenge was good for him. It deflected the sharp edge of his grief and it hastened the development of his own style of resourcefulness. Perhaps of the most importance, each time he successfully negotiated his way through a situation, he could see clearly that he was, indeed, capable, and his trust in himself grew stronger and stronger. The best source of confidence is accomplishment. Not a bristly, overbearing assuredness, no, a real confidence, quiet, patient, watchful.

A few weeks passed and the usual monthly check arrived for his father. Recognizing the envelope as soon as he saw it on the floor, below the mail slot in the door, he picked it up and put it on the table. After looking at the envelope for a while he remembered that a few times he had taken the check to the grocer's after his father had signed it. Merely saying his father wasn't able to get out and around that day was enough information for the grocer to open his register and cash the check. There were never any repercussions: the check always cleared, the father never complained, (it was what he told his son to do,) and so there was no question it was legitimate for the grocer to accept the check.

America knew that to do this now would be dishonest, even criminal. Yet, what was he to do? If he sent the check back with a notation that the payee was deceased, mightn't there be an inquiry? And more to the point of likelihood, what would the merchants come to speculate when Giovanni's checks were no longer being cashed? The money, little as it was, was essential. Yes, there were savings, but his father had taught him carefully that you don't spend savings unless there is absolutely no alternative. Spending savings is a step toward disaster. Not to have as much money as possible in reserve was unthinkable. He went to the corner and, lifting the loose floorboard, he got out the tin box. With the money there were some papers, the lease, his birth certificate, his mother's death certificate, and a small miscellany of short documents. Selecting one from several that bore Giovanni's signature, America sat down to practice writing it as exactly as possible.

This exercise proved to be almost too easy because it was Giovanni himself who had taught his son to write, emphasizing his own penchant for clearly readable letters, round where they should be round, firm vertical strokes where characters needed to be straight, and each i neatly dotted, each t cleanly crossed. With his father's affectionate correcting he overcame the habits Giovanni disapproved of, the unreadable, childish habits which the son had started using, without being noticed, at the school he had attended before they moved here.

When it was a quarter past three Americo went around the corner and down two blocks to the grocer's.

"Good afternoon, Mrs. Quattrocci."

"Hello, Americo. What can I do for you?"

"We need some things, and poppa sent me with his check."

"He's not coming out today?"

"Some days he doesn't walk so good."

"I know. I remember it happened to my father, too. Help yourself. Let me know when you're ready." And she returned to the customer who had been trying to decide between some heads of lettuce.

Mr. Quattrocci was filling in some of the stock on the shelves from large cartons which had recently been delivered. He tilted his head forward to look over his glasses at the boy. "Hello, young fella."

"Hello, Mr. Quattrocci."

"Give your father my regards."

"Yes, sir. Thank you." These pleasantries were easy enough for the boy, and simple exchanges like this helped him to be more relaxed, for a few moments lightening his mood as he lived his masquerade.

When it was his turn Mrs. Quattrocci put his things in a bag and cashed his check. Then Americo crossed the street and before going home stopped at the landlord's door.

"Hello, Mr. Inzerillo. I have the rent." He held out the money.

"Where's Giovanni?"

"You know, some days he doesn't walk so good."

"What does the doctor say?"

"He says it won't get better, and probably will get worse."

"Then there's nothing to do."

"We live with God's will." Again he offered the money and the man accepted it.

"Thank you, Americo. Remember me to Giovanni."

We live with God's will? Why had he said that, he wondered? He had never been to church, nor had his father, who explained he and his family had been union men, and union men could not rely on a fantasy to provide fairness and justice for them. There was no one in the sky who cared if their families were warm and well-fed.

Conversation began to fascinate him, and he was starting to pay a different level of attention to what he said, and what was said to him. After thinking about this exchange he concluded that somehow he simply understood using a common platitude would ease him out of most any conversation, and graciously so. This led to realizing that in conversation people comfortably respond to the slightest misdirecting cues, cues that could be used to bring seemingly idle conversation to a needed point as well as to conclusion. In the neighborhood people wanted to be warm as if they were part of a tribe, but not too close or too personal, and almost never confrontational. There would be casual safety in keeping his words warm and lightly social. He was proud to have discovered a bit of pragmatic wisdom.

He went home and put the money away except for some change. Then he took up his shine-box and went off to get the bus to Forest Hills.

CHAPTER EIGHT

WITHOUT THE LOVE and companionship of his father, it was life itself that became his teacher, and gradually he began to view his experiences very differently than when he was under the close tutelage of his father who had been intensely alert to danger. Situations and actions he had assumed meant one thing little by little revealed to him other meanings, and had other effects on his intelligence and judgment. The teen-aged boys whose shoes he shined began to seem much less interesting, so full of themselves, these children of privilege with their fancy cigarette lighters and key chains, and all of them in their pale blue or light beige cashmere sweaters, the aura they took on, of owning the world. They smelled so clean they must have bathed every day. Didn't they know how much that meant? And if they didn't have to work why weren't they home reading? After nearly three more months of listening to their smart, self-congratulating arrogance he began spending more time in Mr. Battaglia's barber shop, and the bars.

Alone, and very much aware he wasn't an adult, or even a very big kid; he knew he had physical vulnerability. There was little crime in the area, making his father's murder all the more surprising. As intelligent as he was, and insightful as he was becoming, he was, after all, a not quite twelve year old boy, and to compensate for this sense of vulnerability he bought a weight lifting set. He had seen an advertisement in the back of a magazine at the library, Mechanics Illustrated, for this set of equipment. The ad promised that if these weights were used according to the instructions, they would exercise all the important muscle groups, build confidence, (he didn't know he had plenty of that,) and create an appearance of strength, warding off the danger and nuisance of being harassed and embarrassed. He liked that just looking stronger could discourage trouble.

Considering how heavy this equipment must be, it was attractively inexpensive, and besides, the nest egg he had inherited from his father was continuing to grow. At the Post Office he purchased a money order, required by the advertisement, and sent it along with instructions to arrange for a Saturday delivery, when it would be safe for him to answer the door at any time. The heaviness of this material necessitated it be shipped by Railway Express, and delivery was promised for three weeks.

Trips to Forest Hills no longer seemed to be excursions to another country where once he couldn't quite believe he had a right to be, and as he became surer of himself being there wasn't so interesting anymore. His father's death left him without a mentor, and, as if by default, he began thinking without the attachments of his father's social values, which had been freighted with class consciousness learned from his father, the boy's grandfather, who had been an anarchist, in the old country.

In elementary schools, when a subject is being taught, teachers cannot help including undercurrents of social information: prejudices, class distinctions, even political and religious nuances, given in the most incidental and off-hand phrases, all innocently enough during lectures on this or that subject. Americo was exposed to none of this, only his father's views, and he was outgrowing them as he continued his adventures into the world.

The complicated wellsprings of his intellectual and social growth were nourished by his increasingly fearless curiosity, his gifted powers of observation, and the clean directness of his ability to intuit the exquisite simplicity of cause and effect. Time passed and Americo became a little more developed every day, making his way, keeping up the appearances of having an invalid father at home, cashing his father's checks with a monthly forgery, and shining shoes. By now he was nearly twelve, of average height for his age, olive colored skin, large, dark brown eyes, dark-brown curly hair, a pronounced Roman nose, and very strong hands from shining so many shoes. And here was puberty.

His father had given him the basic information but the intensity of the accompanying feelings was unexpected, and here and there confusing. Like when he spoke to Annette, or when he asked a question of the tall, fortyish librarian, who, in answering, would sometimes turn and inadvertently position her large lovely bosom near his face, the neckline of her dress low enough for him to see that her body was very different from his. Then he'd get all warm and fidgety. He started to read about this, too, not quite looking the librarian in the eye when he checked out books that looked like they would help clarify this compelling mystery. When he thought about girls and women his thoughts were of undefined pleasures and learning the miraculous secrets of their bodies, and he wondered about love, about being loved and giving love. He had the thought that when two people were so close and pure in their physical and emotional life that they would be safe.

He stayed home from his shoeshine business the Saturday the weight set was to arrive. It made him take a deep breath when he saw how much larger the wooden crate was than he anticipated as he met the Railway Express driver at the door.

"Ask your mom or dad to come and sign for this. I'll bring the box inside."

"My mother's dead and my father isn't well. He's resting. I'll sign for it and you can leave it right there." He looked the driver directly in the eye, keeping his mind and face devoid of any emotion, with just a hint of a friendly smile.

The driver hesitated. "Okay, kid. But it's heavy." He removed the dolly on which he had wheeled the crate to the door and he was gone.

To get the large amount of heavy material into his home he opened the wooden crate and brought the cast iron weights in one at a time. He read the booklet of instructions, especially the numerous cautions for youthful enthusiasts, and began to work out. Using very light weights he began learning the routines. It all felt comfortable, even the slight aches of muscle growth felt good, and he enjoyed what became his daily one hour workout. Best of all, within a few weeks the aches went away and he began to feel strong.

Feeling stronger he also felt less inclined to keep so minimal a profile when he was away from his home neighborhood. It was time for him to explore the possibilities of a different work environment, to see more of life and of this small part of the world.

CHAPTER NINE

TIRED OF THE trip to Forest Hills, and feeling a mixture of boredom and resentment toward his mostly teen-aged clientele, he decided to get a better look at nearby Elmhurst, and the variety of opportunities he might find there. While not upscale like Forest Hills it was more than a step or two up from the severe poverty of Corona, with a casual mixing of blue and white collar workers. After visiting there just one afternoon he saw that in this relocation his work days would change into an adventure with experiences very new to him. Elmhurst had a less alien personality than the upper middle class Forest Hills and he was comfortable. True, he reasoned, there was no predicting the income possibilities, but it felt good and he wanted to try. If it didn't work out he could go back to those bus trips over the marsh.

He found a number of bars that seemed to do a fair business during the day, and a couple of pool-rooms, also with daytime activity. While he wasn't old enough to be a customer, nor did he have any thoughts to be one, there were no objections to his coming around to work. Actually, he was welcome. In the pool-rooms the money players were meticulous about their appearance, and they liked the idea of having a boy coming around to shine their shoes. It was a small luxury in a world where there were few niceties. And in the bars the daytime habitués saw a shoe-shine as a small expense to lighten their mood. After dinner and into the evening the pool-room and the bars underwent a transformation.

These places became crowded, and for a boy nearly twelve years old this was a very new experience of social life. There was a pulse of excitement that he could never have imagined, no matter how much he might have read about adult life. The printed words he read never captured the smells and the chatter, the subdued lights inside and the glow of neon signs in the windows. The air seemed filled with a soft blanketing murmur of talk, and unless he was near the conversation only an occasional phrase was decipherable. The boy had entered the mysterious world of men at play: gambling, drinking, talking, joking. And in the bars the few women were always smiling, and looking sideways, seductively. Why were they always looking sideways? While he worked he listened and watched.

"Hey, shine-boy, over here." This was said in a friendly drawl. The atmosphere was relaxed, and these people liked the curly-haired boy with the olive skin and the wide, easy smile. And in this part of the city, more prosperous than Corona but still poorer by far than Forest Hills, almost every customer gave him a quarter. The men were mostly Italian, with now and then a few Chinese. There were some dark skinned families in the neighborhood, and they all got along well enough, but they and the Italians didn't mingle.

Working fairly steadily he soon became a part of the texture of the bar and pool-room life in the area. He was a kid earning a few bucks, quiet in his manner, unobtrusive, delivering a nice shine whenever he was asked. There was never an unpleasant incident involving either him or his services, and he managed to keep working without attracting much notice or anyone asking probing questions. He was just a shoe-shine boy who one day showed up and without much ado became part of the local scene.

He came across a bakery, Tramontana's, where the baker's wife made sandwiches to order, using bread fresh from the oven. She would split open a small loaf, smear a little mustard on the steaming, soft hot whiteness, and over that put five thin slices of a choice of cold-cuts and a splash of olive oil. For Americo the cold meat usually was hard Italian salami, with black peppercorns scattered throughout, and when the salami went through the electric slicer the peppercorns would be sliced, too, and he savored that touch of sharpness. This was ten cents, and a soda was five more. He was very pleased to find this place, and regarded this discovery as another accomplishment.

It was the first winter without his father, and the holidays were coming. Holidays had meant little to his father, Giovanni, except that on holidays Americo didn't have to stay out of sight and could work a full day. Yet the boy was very much aware of the effect the comings and goings of holidays had on other people, and he knew these would be good times for bigger tips. He himself never entered into the spirit of the celebrations, he just liked the different decorations for the various occasions, and the smiling felicities that even strangers at these times would exchange. The merry Christmases, and the smiling good-natured bursts of Happy New Years were pleasant seasonal street sounds. And, soon enough, with March he would observe the first anniversary of his father's murder. He had been working in Elmhurst for two months.

One evening, as he was walking after dinner toward a pool-room, a tall black-skinned man leaning against a building called to him. "Hey, shine-boy, c'mere." Americo tensed, and looked at the man. "C'mere. Gimme a 'shine. Show me what you know." He held out a quarter, and Americo, with some wariness, (he was always paid after he did his work), walked over to him, put his box down, took the quarter and set to work.

As he tapped the man's foot to let him know he was finished the man said, "Now, you give me a quarter and I'll shine your shoes, and you'll learn something!" His voice was soft and deep, and unhurriedly melodious.

Americo looked at the man with as much a question in his mind as there was on his face. The guy seemed okay to him, his casual friendliness appeared genuine, as if he really wanted to show him something. And his curiosity was definitely piqued by the man's apparently open and uncomplicated directness. He stood up and gave the man the quarter he had just earned, and they changed places. Very soon Americo's eyes widened with appreciation as the man went at his scuffed, worn shoes with a deft and graceful energy.

"Boy," he said, "Now this is how you do pop-the-cloth. You pay attention, now." And he made the rag snap like a whip, and the worn scuffed shoes started to sparkle.

"Now watch close. You spit just a little bit on the toe cap." And he spit a little bit on Americo's toe cap. "Now watch what happens." And as he snapped and popped the rag the toe caps looked like small stars on his feet.

The man stood up, smiled, and asked, "What's your name, boy?"

"Americo," he replied. "What's yours?"

"I been hearing you were around. You've made some friends here and you probably don't even know that, do you?"

The boy nodded a negative.

"Frankie. You can call me Big Frank." And they shook hands.

"You're good, Big Frank."

"Yeah, I know a few things. Now you go and make yourself some money. You shine 'em like this you'll be famous around here." He reached out and affectionately rubbed the boy's dark curly head.

Americo took his shine-box and walked away, mulling over what Big Frank had said, and the manner of his speaking. There was a comfort in this meeting, a comfort that pleased him, and he wondered if they would be friends.

He went to Ed's Pool Hall where the more serious games were played. The place was known among good players throughout the city, and almost any evening some of them, from the Bronx, or Brooklyn, or "the city," would stop by and find each other, and play sometimes for as much as five dollars a game. The hangers-on knew enough to appreciate the skills they were watching, and they would softly tap on the floor at any unusual show of skill. At times they applauded.

Americo soon learned never to set up for business near a serious match, and this evening looked plenty serious. He wanted to watch one of the games, but he also wanted to make money, and he could see this was not the right time. After a moment he backed away. As he turned to the stairs Ed, the owner, came over and patted him on the shoulder, and said to come back the next night. Ed liked him to come around.

He went to a bar, Jacquie's Place, and found a pleasant enough social evening in progress. It was really a café with chairs and tables and a limited menu. Mostly it was a drink place. There were some colored neon lights in the windows, and a few more on the walls, and two dim ceiling lights. The space was filled with cigarette smoke, and the sound of people having a good time. Not loudly, just feeling good together.

He was called to work almost as he entered. "Shine-boy. Over here." He put to work his new found knowledge and the reaction was immediate.

"Hey, shine-boy, you learned something new."

"Shine, that's a real shine!"

He was busier than ever and stayed quite late. He made a lot of money, maybe twelve dollars, as some customers gave him half dollars and one a whole dollar.

He was proud of his successful evening, the praise he had received and the wad of money in his pocket filled him with new levels of satisfaction. His life had become mostly focused on a succession of challenges, and as he met them he felt a constant growth of confidence. But it was only the bare needs of survival to which he was measuring up. Tonight he learned about a new experience of accomplishment, he learned about personal excellence and from that something better than ever before: pride. All during the trip home his spirits were raised, almost joyful, until he closed the door behind him, and stood quietly in the dark, empty room and whispered, "Oh, poppa."

CHAPTER TEN

THE NEXT DAY, after he finished reading, and it was after three o'clock, he went out to run a few errands: grocery shopping and the library. At the library, as it often happened, he ran into Annette, and he felt good seeing her. After asking about her, and her father's newsstand, he told her about the bakery he discovered, and asked if they could go there together after school, or on a Saturday. They could get sandwiches and sodas and go into the little near-by park and sit on one of the benches next to the pond. He wanted to be with her, to eat and talk. He envisioned sitting by the pond and feeling good as they had lunch together.

She blushed, and smiled, pleased to be invited, but she couldn't miss any of the time when she was needed to work with her father. While many men still worked a six day week, more and more Saturday was becoming a half day. Even so, Saturday was a good day for selling newspapers at their location, and she and her father had to be there starting at noon.

Americo smiled at her, a twelve year old boy's large, first-love smile, and she smiled again, and they went where they each had to go.

He walked three blocks to a dry goods store and bought a few pairs of inexpensive socks, then to a candy store where he got a package of loose-leaf paper to practice writing, a few pencils, and some gum, because he had never had any and wanted to try a package, if only to see what it was like.

The sky had gotten silvery gray, and it had started to drizzle while he was in the candy store. He hadn't brought his raincoat and he had no love for getting wet, but having taken enough time for errands he wanted to get back to work. For forty cents he bought a canvas book bag, explaining to himself that aside from the rain he really needed it. Putting the library books and his purchases in the bag, and tucking the small brown bag of groceries under the other arm, (one eye searching the sky for signs of brightness in the west, hoping the sun would return,) he started for home to put everything away and get his shine-box.

As he neared the corner he saw a crowd of people in the street, and some cars stopped in an odd manner in the middle of where there would normally be traffic. The cars were at a standstill, and the crowding pedestrians, some in windbreakers, some in raincoats, stood quietly, not milling as one would expect from a crowd in the street. It was unpleasantly quiet.

The crowd of people was looking toward their center, at something they were surrounding. As Americo got closer he heard a few people at the fringe talking about "the accident," and he heard the word "dead." There came a terrible pain in his stomach, and he began to sweat and feel icy cold. He pushed and wiggled through the crowd, and being shorter than the gathered adults he was easily able to get to the accident and see what had happened.

For some moments the boy couldn't breathe, or hear, or even think. His brain stopped as he looked at the violent, tragic death scene. He took deep breaths as he looked at the body. His heart was still beating fast even after realizing he had been overcome with dread, thinking the victim was Annette. It embarrassed him how hugely he was relieved to see it was only a young woman, a stranger to him, lying on the wet pavement, a thin streak of blood near her mouth, her skin ashen. These feelings of relief startled him.

Holding his book bag and grocery package tightly, he hurried home, the tears in his eyes barely under control. He put the groceries away, opened one of the folding cots, removed his shoes, and lay face down on the bed, only then letting himself cry. He pulled the blanket around him, and sobbed and cried well into the evening, at last opening up, sobbing and crying for his departed father, whom he had loved so much and who had been so much of his world. And he cried for his confusing love of Annette, and then for himself, for his loneliness, his isolation, his need to be constantly vigilant to protect his freedom, his way of life that even with many problems and pains was dear to him. When he finally fell into a light sleep the rain had begun coming down harder. Almost from when they had first moved here he was at ease with the sound of raindrops on the tin roof. This evening as he slept he was aware of the soft reassuring pattering with the delicate ping of each drop, reminders of a more protected, safer time. The rain continued, its rhythm taking him into a deep, deep sleep.

It was a rare evening when he didn't go to work but his mind and soul were aching, and he had no will to struggle any longer with his overwhelming sadness. He let his mind flow into his heart's sorrowful weariness without reservation. In the morning he awoke and washed, but couldn't manage any food. He didn't leave his home for two more days. Mostly he cried, drank sweet tea, and thought about Annette, and his father, and his life. He cried the tears he needed to cry until he was able to think again. He decided that he liked his life, the ways of his days and evenings, his easy manner of keeping everything going, but he was terribly, terribly lonely, and he understood that the real joy of accomplishment and success is having someone dear with whom to share the goodness.

On the third day he knew he was regaining the strength of his will when he decided it was time to resume his normal routine. He worked out for an hour with his weights, and then he read until noon, had sandwiches for lunch, read again, until three, and took his shine box and headed for Elmhurst, reflecting on Annette, and the depth of his distress when he had thought she might be hurt, or even dead. He hardly knew her and she had become so important to him.

As he walked he saw three boys approaching. He could tell right away they were a little older than he was, and he could also see that none of them were as strong as he had become. They were walking straight toward him.

"Hey," one of them said. "Ain't seen you here before."

"I haven't seen you, either." He backed away a step so that

he could face all three of them without being surrounded.

"What's your name?"

They didn't appear to be looking for trouble.

"Americo. Who are you?"

"I'm Tony T. Then he pointed to his friends, "Gianni and Vincent." They each shook hands. Gianni turned to spit in the street.

Pointing to the shine box Vincent asked, "Goin' to work?"

"Don't you work?"

"We work at the yard."

"We're goin' there now," said Gianni; he turned to spit in the street again.

"Yard?"

"The lumber yard."

"You guys old enough for papers?"

"Nah. Old man Liberto pays us off the books. We just do odd stuff. Kinda heavy."

"Oh."

"How's the shine business?"

"Okay, I guess."

"Goin' to Yankee Stadium Sunday, after church. Wanna come?"

"What's there?"

"A baseball game! The Yankees! You never been to a base ball game?"

The boys were surprised. Gianni turned and spit again.

"C'mon. It'll be good."

"The Red Sox are in town."

"I have to work," he lied, there being no place even worth trying to work on a Sunday.

"Don't your old man give you any time off?"

"Yeah. What does your mom say?"

"My mom's dead."

"Oh. Sorry."

They stood silent for a moment.

"Well, we gotta get to the job."

"Me too."

Americo was of mixed thoughts. It was nice to be approached in friendship. And with this route to his new working territory he might be seeing them again. They were friendly, but he didn't want to be friends with them. He didn't dislike them, it was just that though they were older they seemed like kids and in their presence he felt much older and more mature: he was wiser and in their company he was a grown-up. And, although he couldn't work on Sundays, if he were to take time off from reading or walking, or only resting, he would rather be with Annette. Will she ever have time for him? Will they ever smile together, would he ever hold her in his arms?

He continued on his way, past the bus stop. Today he would take a brisk walk. The sky was still gray, but not threatening, and he passed a house where an old man he knew only as Mr. Ianucci lived, who kept pigeons in a coop on his flat roof. As Americo passed he saw old man Ianucci on the roof, directing his flock of pigeons with a long pole he waived in slow circles, his birds swirling around and around, dipping and cresting in the gray sky. He waved at Americo and the boy waved back.

CHAPTER ELEVEN

AT ED'S POOL HALL he put in three hours of good work and went to dinner. There wasn't a big game but there were some money players there who were practicing and being social without the pressure of confrontation. They got shines while they smoked and drank coffee, and they gossiped about games they had seen in this town or that. Good players whose skills stood up under the pressure of high stakes had among themselves a brotherhood, a fraternity of acknowledged respect for each other even as they competed. The room was quiet during their big games, the atmosphere tense as their abilities were pushed to the limit. Their level of play was beautiful to watch, and Americo had begun to understand enough about the mechanics and strategy of the game to appreciate what he was seeing. Mostly he didn't watch, wisely concentrating on his own business.

His savings were growing steadily, and he was thinking that tonight he'd treat himself to a real dinner. Several times he had passed a diner, and he had thought about going in. Now he would give it a try.

The interior was cozy and bright with lots of shiny chrome trim, and green and black tiles on the floor. The air inside almost dizzied him with hunger-inducing aromas of steaming hot food, not something he had had much of since his mother died. As he passed the cushioned booths he decided he'd be more at ease at the counter. The waitress brought him a glass of water and a menu, the first menu he had ever held. There was so much from which to choose. The overwhelming assortment of choices left Americo momentarily thoughtless. He thought everything looked like it might be pretty good. As he read he reflected with some grandiosity that if this meal was good he'd come back to try something else. And, if the food kept being good maybe he would eventually try all the dishes they offered. "How about that?" he said to himself, his foot resting against his shine box, on the floor next to his seat. With his growing success he always had a couple of dollars in his pocket, even before he started work for the day. He had become an odd combination of capitalist and proletarian.

"It makes things easier if you have a little money," he mused to himself. He still worked hard, and pretty much followed the regimen laid down by his strict father. But he was gradually, carefully, relaxing the extreme Spartan self-denial he grew up with. He was earning more money, and, with his expenses staying mostly constant, his savings were growing substantially.

He ordered veal stew over rice, and it came with a side of

spinach. It was hot. He thought this was a truly excellent event, having a real dinner, a hot food dinner. It was good, and he busied himself with this wonderful meal. As he ate, careful not to rush this mildly momentous event, a friendly hand touched his shoulder.

"Big Frank."

"Americo. I see you're doin' all right for yourself."

"I'm doing okay. How are you?"

"Fine, fine." He looked at the boy's plate. "How's the stew?"

"Nice."

Frankie turned to the waitress, who had just put down a glass of water and a menu. "Hello, Angie. I'll have the same as my little friend, here."

"I hear you been doin' good shines around here lately."

"You taught me good." He smiled and chewed.

"Well, you're just a workin' stiff, and a kid at that. I'd been hearing good things about you here and there, and I figured, well, I'd give you a little boost."

"You know, after you showed me, and I did good, it was easier."

Frankie smiled at the boy.

"I was working harder, and it was easier. How come?"

"You're a smart boy. You'll figure it out."

The boy ate slowly, savoring the food carefully. The man ate quickly.

"Sorry I can't stay for dessert. I gotta get someplace. See you around, my little friend."

"Okay, Big Frank, I'll see you around."

He finished the meal and topped it off with an over-sized

black and white cookie and a cup of light coffee, with many spoonfuls of sugar. When he went to the cashier he learned that Big Frank had paid for him on his way out.

CHAPTER TWELVE

AND THAT'S HOW it went for the boy. The days were occupied with reading and working, learning more about the world, and about himself, too. He began reading discarded newspapers which he found in street trash baskets. If there was a clean one he'd take it home. While he was spending more he was still careful with money, and all his expenditures were thoughtfully considered. When his spending was a little looser it was for better food.

Once or twice a week he would run into Annette, either at the library or on the street. Their conversations were held on to, noticeably drawn out, ending with each of them blushing slightly, and their spirits lighter. One afternoon, after Annette had left the library, Americo, as was his custom, went into the stacks to find a few books. As he selected one and placed it on a near-by table he saw there was already a book left lying there, and with no one else around it appeared to have been idly abandoned. He picked it up and read the title, "World Poetry in Translation." He had read references to poetry but had never felt impelled to read any. Leafing through the pages his eye was caught by some lines, and he stopped to read.

> *"I believe that star*
> *these thousand years is dead,*
> *though I still see its light."*

And further,

> *"One of all these stars*
> *must still exist.*
> *I believe I know*
> *which one*
> *still lasts*
> *and stands like a city, white*
> *in the sky at the end of the beam of light..."*

"How so few words can be so large," he reflected, touched by the beauty of what he had read. "But it makes what I care about so small, so unimportant. No, I am more than that. I am important," he insisted to himself. "Maybe not to anyone else, but I am important to me!" He found the words beautiful and moving, but it didn't dissuade him from his self-interest, and what he needed to do, every day. He decided however, to borrow the book along with the other book he had selected. And then he took two more, one for himself and one for the pretense of still having a father.

As he was leaving he noticed a new acquisition for this branch, a globe of the world on a stand in a far corner of the reading room. He went over and rotated it, looking at the countries and oceans he had read about. Then he searched for Corona, which, of course, was too small to be included on the globe. He did find New York City and Long Island, and guessed at the spot where he might be standing at this very moment. It seemed very tiny, and as he walked away he turned and looked back, the whole concept of space and distances appeared daunting and depressive, definitely not as sadly attractive as in the poem he had just read.

On a street near one of the pool-rooms he had noticed a barber shop, and made a note to go in there some afternoon. The bars and the pool-rooms were keeping him very busy after dinner. In the afternoons, however, business was spotty: sometimes middling good, sometimes only fair to poor. He was looking to add another afternoon location and the barbershop looked promising, always busy. Often there were customers that had to wait. Yet he had been hesitating: the barber looked tough in an unpleasant way, and he doubted he would be comfortable in such a man's company. After passing by a number of times over a few weeks, and each time glancing in, he finally entered and inquired. It was a four chair shop and the proprietor, Mr. Abruzezze, thought it might be all right for the boy to work there, but they should do a two week trial.

"Come in tomorrow afternoon, we'll see how it goes." After a moment's thought he asked, "How much you charge?"

"Ten cents a shine."

"I think maybe they pay more in my shop because it's convenient. They get a haircut, they get a shave, they get a shine. You charge fifteen cents and give me a nickel for each shine."

Americo stared at the man without answering.

"Okay?" Mr. Abruzezze asked, impatiently.

This shop was noisier than the one in Forest Hills, the barbers and their customers chatting away about horses and odds. Mr. Abruzezze ran a small book and there was a steady exchange of slips of paper and folded one dollar bills. The shop was consistently working at capacity, and about half the customers asked for a shine. At the end of the first week Mr. Abruzezze brought in a low stool for Americo to sit on while he worked, and for the short intervals when he would be waiting for work.

Shining shoes in the evenings was very different from work in the afternoons. After dinner the world he worked in was more serious, and he had to be careful. When men were playing pool for money, or drinking with each other, and with women around, he quickly understood there was a fine line separating the sociability of a good time from the barely tolerant moments that could envelop a man while he was drinking or losing money. With the mix of alcohol and women a man could turn on a dime, from civility to anger, and sometimes from anger to sudden explosive rage. Corona was a safe family neighborhood, Elmhurst was not.

About the anger he saw, and the violence he avoided seeing, he pondered just how unreasonable or unexpected it was. He almost always sensed it coming, and managed to never to be too close when things got hot.

Over the next several weeks, he learned that in the evenings there was an atmosphere of danger even when things were going smoothly. The mix of booze, money and women made some men edgy, even as they were laughing and dancing. The bars all had juke boxes, the sound turned to a moderate level, and at a nickel per tune big band music was the usual bouncy sound that the customers selected. He didn't stay late enough to hear the sad ballads, or see the faces of the left-over men smoking and drinking alone after the women decided with whom they would leave.

Frankie was a friend who appeared unpredictably. He was always glad to see him, and when they met they talked easily, about the street life around them, the action in the poolrooms, the life in the bars. He didn't get advice from him as much as he got interesting questions, questions that had him thinking about why we do what we do. Frankie never asked about his personal life, nor did he offer any information about his own, or what he did for a living. Americo knew he should never ask, but he sometimes wondered. Money never seemed to be an issue with the man. He was relaxed, with an easy manner, and wise about many of the things that appealed to the boy's curiosity. Like the boy, Frankie was intensely alert. It was Americo's private hunch that Frankie was a thief, but he really didn't know. He liked that Frankie was his friend.

His twelfth birthday came and he gave himself a day off from everything except caution. The night before he bought the next morning's newspaper, and when he awoke in the morning he made breakfast, turned on his radio, and drank sweet tea and read the paper from cover to cover. (The tide of the war had turned in our favor.) He still dared not venture out during school hours, or go near the window.

After lunch he thought about his father. It filled him with an eerie blend of sadness and pleasure to reflect on how much Giovanni had loved him, how he had been the center of so much of his father's thinking, and how his main focus had been to foster his son's well-being, to keep him from the "system."

He thought about his father's values, aware that while he still followed many of his precepts he had also improved on the life they shared. He felt less fear in his conversations with neighborhood merchants, he had a friend in Big Frank, he was eating better, and his savings had grown to quite a nice little sum, more than two hundred dollars.

With more experience and thoughtfulness there were new questions. What would become of him as he grew into manhood? Would he shine shoes all his life? How would he learn to do something more complicated? What would it be like to be older and no longer have to restrict himself from being anything more than slightly visible?

What he was musing about was at least four years away, and while these thoughts were important he only returned to them from time to time. He had taken the afternoon off but when dinnertime came Americo became restless. He picked up his shine box and left for Elmhurst, and the diner. This time Frankie was already eating. He sat down next to his friend and they shook hands.

"How ya doin' today, Shine?" It seemed that almost from the first day he picked up his shoeshine box his work had become the name he was known by.

"Oh, fine, I guess. Yourself?"

"I'm good."

The waitress came with water and a menu.

"Miss Angie, is that lasagna?" He pointed to Big Frank's plate. Americo had learned her name but she wasn't very talkative, no matter his shy warmth and good smile.

"Um, yeah."

"I'll have that, too. And some tea."

"Uh-oh. Better bring some more sugar."

"And some ketchup, please."

"Shine, it's got tomato sauce on it!"

"Might not be enough. What do you think?"

"I think you're one odd little fella."

They sat and ate, chatted and lightly laughed.

"Where you shinin' tonight?"

"Over at Jacquie's."

"Be careful. There's a real bad guy there now."

"Yeah?"

"I'm not kiddin' you, my little friend."

"Who's this guy?"

"Luigi Leopardi. He's bad, bad, bad."

"Have I seen him before?"

"He's been outta town."

"I'll be careful."

"Don't get too close." "What's with him?"

"He's a snake."

CHAPTER THIRTEEN

AMERICO PICKED UP his shine box, put a dime tip on the counter, and went to the cashier to pay. Then he walked over to Jacquie's.

Entering as quietly as he could, he stayed on the fringes of the crowd, his smile lighting his way among the outer tables. There was a "Hey, Shine, over here," and he was at work. There were familiar men and women seated at the tables, only tonight the sound levels of the conversations in the room were much softer, unnaturally subdued compared to the bouncy lilt of the music from the juke box. Three or four couples were dancing, and they, too, appeared strange, moving slower than the music's tempo. While they were all drinking, smoking and talking, there was a sense they were not quite enjoying themselves, a feeling of hesitance in the air, a vague aura of restraint.

He understood from the very first day he began shining

shoes that he should never stare at anyone, and to keep eye contact at a minimum. After working a while he noticed the tips were a little off. The customers still gave him quarters, but there were no half dollars, or more, which, in his experience, was the norm among men in a bar where there were women. Still, the men liked having their foot up on his shine-box while they chatted with each other and their women, and smoked and drank.

As he worked, and made his way around the room, he covertly glanced at the men in the further parts of the large bar-room, trying to see this Luigi fellow. At the tables he saw the regulars, faces that were there often enough to be familiar. Against the bar there were some men talking, with one given a little more room than the others. He was one of the few who wore a suit and a hat. As Americo looked in his direction the man removed his hat and, placing it on the bar, he turned to look over the room, checking if there were any women who caught his fancy. He had the self-assuredness that if he found a woman appealing she would leave the man she was with and come to drink on his dime.

As Luigi turned to survey the female talent in the room Americo could see his face and in an instant his long-practiced cautious self-control was shockingly disrupted as at first he stared and then could only gape! No, can it be! This was the man who murdered his father! Leopardi was the man in the alley who stabbed his father in the back, the man who, in one vicious act, ended his dear sweet father's life! The boy turned deathly pale and stopped breathing as the blood drained from his swarthy face.

"Hey, Shine, you having a heart attack?"

"What?"

"My shoes, boy."

"Oh."

Trying not to tremble he resumed work on the man's shoes, buffing vigorously to raise his energy and get his blood flowing again. He didn't need to look in Luigi's direction any more, not this night. There was no mistaking who he was. It was that man, he, the sneaky predator who had taken from him his one loving connection in this whole world, leaving him too much alone, and much too much in silence. The pain of loss had slowly, gradually diminished, especially as his attention was continuously directed to the daily challenges of his life, but the loneliness was persistent, and the silence was there in the long hours when he was in his room, even with the radio on.

His shock had quickly become anger, and this he knew was good because anger he could control. He worked hard, smiling, and thanking his customers. Most of the men had often been previous customers at one time or another. Now he was into his work, and worked well and moved around the room slowly while his mind was racing, teeming with thoughts and images the meaning of which he was not ready to fathom. Some of the pretty women, as he passed near them, or worked on their companion's shoes, would run a hand through his curly dark mop of hair. He liked that, and he liked feeling angry, and he saw how much he liked having a great anger that was in his control. He felt the illusion of an enormous power in his secret knowledge. A venomous secrecy! What a discovery!

This evening he worked later than usual, his energy level strong and inspired. He was in control, like a playwright. He had an angry secret and now he was on a stage, starring in his own play, at once both the writer and the only member of the audience. No one else suspected what was happening, that there was a play in progress, and at its center a masterful performance. And the extras? They didn't know they were in a cast, and, well, as the playwright he would work it out whatever way he needed to, improvising and maneuvering the unwitting members of what had now become his company. He didn't know the whole plot yet, he just knew there was a drama that had begun and he was confident he would find resolution. He knew. And in his youthful naïveté he was enjoying some self-indulgent grandiosity.

"Hey, boy! Shine." It was Luigi, and the first of a number of small moments of truth. Americo never hesitated; he was in control of his initial shock at the horrifying recognition. He stood up and brought his box over to the man, who put his foot upon the narrow wooden block of a footrest on top of the box, (built by his father!) and the boy put his thin horse hair filled pillow on the floor and went to work. Luigi stood with his back to the bar, his elbows resting on the bar-top, and when Americo looked up with his best smile the man was preoccupied in conversation with some acquaintances. He spoke in a quiet voice, with the smug smirk of a powerful man who has always had things his way, and who knew he was feared. He was confident in his shrewd, constant vigilance, his careful awareness of his surroundings, in his ability to be violent, and even kill. This confidence insulated him from having any thought that while this boy was shining his shoes it was he himself who was in danger.

Americo popped the cloth and spit a small spray on the toe caps and brought the man's shoes to a sparkle that was better than any he had ever done, likely because these were the most expensive shoes he had ever worked on. Luigi was a sport and was careful about his appearance. Americo tapped the man's shoe on the side, signaling that he was finished. Luigi looked down and grinned with deep pleasure.

"Boy, you are something!"

"Thank you."

"What's the most anyone ever give you, boy?"

"A dollar, mister."

"A dollar? For a shine like this? Here's a five, boy."

Luigi, putting on a show, handed him the five with a little flourish. It was more money than he stole when he murdered the boy's father. It was all Americo could do not to burst into tears at the shame of it.

"Thank you, mister," he managed in a hoarse whisper, his hand ever so slightly trembling as he accepted the bill.

Luigi assumed the boy was moved by his big-time gesture, and everyone close enough to have seen the transaction was smiling and feeling better.

"Tonight, boy, you shined Mister Luigi's shoes."

"Thank you."

"You won't forget me too soon, now will you?"

"No, Mr. Luigi, I'll remember you for a long time."

Having regained control over his moment of deep emotion, he gave the man his best smile, again. He knew it was his best smile because lately he had been watching himself in the mirror at the barbershop. At this Luigi began smiling, too, and everybody liked to see Luigi smiling, and all the patrons present couldn't help but join in as the low, underlying tension in the room finally dissipated, to everyone's noticeable relief.

Americo picked up his box and made his way out of Jacquie's, where, in the clear evening air, he was relieved to be on the street alone with his thoughts. He took the bus on Roosevelt Avenue to a stop about sixteen blocks from his home, to give him the chance to have something of a calming walk. He was thinking, but there was too much to think about for the boy to have much clarity, and he hoped he would not be in too much turmoil to get a good night's sleep. As he lay in bed he thought of his father's ring which Luigi was wearing on his left pinkie.

Chapter Fourteen

Americo stayed within his normal routine, working out and reading in the mornings, having lunch, then reading again until three, going out and running an errand or two, if needed, and then leaving for Elmhurst to work at his usual places until dinner time. But after eating he made sure to work at Jacquie's only every third or fourth evening. He wanted to be careful; to be sure he would not be noticed as having reacted to the arrival of one Luigi Leopardi.

If he happened to see Annette at the library he was still pleased, and her smile still made his heart smile, but he no longer mentioned meeting for lunch, nor were their whispered conversations as drawn out. She noticed this and was concerned that he didn't like her as much as she thought he had, and when they spoke there was some sadness within her. With his recent discovery Americo had only one focus.

One of the books he borrowed from the library was a large volume on anatomy. He needed to know the exact location of the heart, how deep it was in the chest cavity, and its accessibility. He was relieved that he was right-handed, and that the heart of a man facing him would be somewhat more on his right, where his main strength was. Then he determined how long a knife would have to be to effectively reach through the ribs and kill that heart, at the same time making note of at what angle and approximately between which ribs.

From a book on combat he learned to hold a knife like a sword and use it to thrust. This was more effective than holding it like a dagger and trying to stab, a motion much easier to defend. He went to an Army and Navy store in Elmhurst that he had passed a number of times. Standing at the counter he studied the various sheathed knives, and asked if he could see one. The man behind the counter didn't like his question.

"Why's a kid like you need a knife like that?"

"It's a gift for my father's birthday."

"What, he's a hunter?"

"He likes to whittle."

"Is that a fact." This last was a statement, not a question.

"I have some money, and I know he'd like that one." Saying this, Americo drew a few dollars from his pocket. Business hadn't been much this last week and the sight of money had the man's attention.

"How much is that one?"

The man took it from the display case and turned it over to look at the tag.

"A buck fifty, kid."

"Here. Can you wrap it?"

"This is an Army-Navy. You get a brown bag."

Americo nodded. After paying he put the bag with the knife under the cans of polish at the bottom of his shoe-shine box, and went on to Jacquie's.

He had become a first-rate shine-boy, giving truly superb shines, and he liked shining shoes, listening to his customers' bantering, the women rubbing his curly-haired head, the music in the background. He went at it with a good-natured zest that put everyone at ease. Even with his advancing expertise and his evolving social development, he never allowed himself into conversation with customers, and they could put their attention elsewhere, not having to respond to anything he might say. He loved listening to their conversations, and when their talk turned to Luigi, as it often did, the words he most often heard were "snake," and "dangerous," and "don't get too close."

When Luigi was there Americo would only watch him from side glances, and never dare to risk tipping his hand by looking at him directly. He noticed one of the man's favorite positions at the bar was to face the room and lean against the mahogany with both elbows back upon the top surface supporting his relaxed weight. His key observation was that whenever someone flattered him, and did so with some catchy attempt at wit, he would laugh with his head tilted back, leaning more heavily on his elbows, with his chest pushed forward just enough to leave him as perfectly vulnerable as could be wished.

He gauged Luigi's height at about five foot eleven, and his target area at about level with Americo's own shoulders. At home he put a mark on one wall at about that heart's height, and he set up his shine box before that mark, as if Luigi were standing there, getting his shoes shined. He put his sheath knife on his belt, positioned at his back, above his right buttock and under his sweater, which was long enough to keep the sheath hidden, even as he was bent over while working. He practiced a quick draw with a forceful, angled thrust at the mark on the wall. At first he was clumsy and slow. The hilt would catch in his sweater, or his grip would be too high. He was surprised at the many little parts of this act that could go wrong. It was a straightforward thing he wanted to do, and he learned that even this kind of work demanded a practiced technique. With time and effort he knew he would get it right. He would eventually be able to take hold of the knife, rise from his kneeling work stance, and thrust into the mark, all in one lightning-quick, well-practiced, smooth, powerful stroke.

He worked at this a half hour in the morning and another half hour in the late evening, before going to bed. Whenever he tried to think of exactly when he would do this deed he would back off. He knew there would be only one chance and he had better do it well.

He purchased a cheap calendar for six cents and marked the days as they passed. He would mark a day ten days hence, and prepare for that, and then back off when confronted by the fearful actuality of what he was planning to do. He began to anticipate the discomfort of those mornings, those arbitrarily chosen mornings when he awoke, looked at the calendar, and a rush of anxiety would tighten his stomach, and then nausea.

His hatred for Luigi Leopardi never lessened, and in his determination to avenge his father's murder he never wavered. In his planning his feelings were cool, employing both his instincts and his intelligence to their capacity. But killing a man was so wrong, so sure and definite a step over the boundaries of law and morality, that when he determined that this day, today, was the day it would be done, he became rattled and distraught with great physical distress, an unbearable condition he could only ease by backing off from his plan.

Americo began to wonder if he could really do this. In his fantasy he stalked his prey as if he were a giant hawk and Luigi a helpless, unsuspecting mouse about to become his dinner. But, face to face with the prospect of acting out this fantasy, Luigi was the deadly giant, and he, Americo, the small creature, a child with dramatic delusions gleaned from too much reading while in loneliness and grief.

What he was less conscious of was that since finding Luigi and developing a plan of vengeance, his life had become more animated: his heart beat stronger, he awoke each morning with a driving, consuming purpose, and his mind ran at full-throttle, thinking with a raised and constant focus. If he killed this mortal enemy what would there be to look forward to that could energize his thoughts and actions at this level? Heretofore his driving force was propelled by an intellectually gifted boy's curiosity, and his father's crafty teachings about survival. Fantasizing on preparing Luigi's death gave his life an inner, volcanic animation.

Sometimes when sleeping he dreamed of his father talking to him from another world. In these dreams it was never clear what his father was saying; only that he was talking to him in a manner that was definitely reproachful. On awakening he would wonder, was the reproach for his plotting an awful murder, or was it for his fearfulness at carrying out this plan?

Chapter Fifteen

"Hello, Big Frank."

"How are you, Americo?"

"Okay. You?"

"All is good, little friend."

Americo nodded.

"I've been hearing good things about you. You're a shine demon, they say."

"I've been working."

"You've been working, alright. You must have some package by now."

"Package?"

"Money."

"I need a favor, Big Frank."

"Talk to me."

"Tonight, when I finish work, could you take my shine-box

and keep it until tomorrow afternoon, about three-thirty?"

Big Frank looked at the boy thoughtfully.

"Sure." He wanted to know more but he wouldn't ask, and he understood Americo was not about to be forthcoming. Frankie from their first meeting saw the boy as more than a little different from what a young boy should be. He also was wise enough to know there was a shadow, and for some instinctive reason which he couldn't quite define, he felt there was an elusive connection to the snake Luigi.

The boy's plan was to learn more about Luigi and his habits. He had no specific reason or detailed purpose; his motive was only that it seemed a good thing to do. That night he worked a normal evening, sweating over shoes as he worked with an energy powered by an amalgam of anger and anxiety, and an indecisive desperation.

After nine o'clock he left and found Frankie walking up the street, toward him. He handed him his shine-box.

"Thanks, Big Frank."

Wordlessly Frankie took the box and nodded a farewell, and Americo turned and walked away.

When he got to the corner he turned into the next street where, out of sight, he stopped. He went back to the corner and peeked around it. Frankie had left, and there were only three or four people on the street, going in different directions, with nothing in particular about any of them. The street was dark, and there were many shadows in which to hide if there was anyone who needed to remain unobserved.

The idea of this exercise was exciting and fraught with both fake melodrama and real peril, but it proved dull and without any value. After waiting two boring hours in the concealment of a dark doorway's shadow, he finally saw Luigi emerge from Jacquie's with an attractive woman in a light–colored skirt, making them easy to follow. Kissing and laughing, they walked for a couple of blocks until they entered a dark building on a dark street. A minute later a light went on two floors up. Then it went out, and the adventure was over. He hadn't even learned if the building was where Luigi lived or where the woman lived. And he wasn't sure it mattered. He felt like a dumb kid playing a stupid game. Here he was, in a momentous situation of life and death, a true saga of heartbreak, vengeance and justice, and the best he could do was to go hiding in shadows while his enemy, his prey, was pursuing a little fun.

He did learn how easy it was to follow someone, especially someone who had no reason to consider they were being followed. On the way home this knowledge translated into his worrying there might be someone following him. He feared he might have been seen, and his activity discovered. There were people who knew he was making good money now, and with a wad of money in his pocket he could be a target. And while someone was watching him they would discover his strange behavior stalking Luigi, and maybe sell him that surprising information. He reminded himself that one mistake and he would be dead. Thankfully, when he got on the bus no one else boarded with him, and as the bus pulled away he stared out the back window at the street. There would be no more of this foolishness.

The next morning, tired from his late night out and the exhausting tension his activity had produced, he slept in, not waking until half the morning had passed.

He rose and worked out, washed and had breakfast, all the while thinking hard, trying to be more clear-headed. His decision was to stay with what was familiar, to resume his normal routine and not get too fancy or dramatic. "Something will happen," he said to himself, "and I will be ready, and know what to do."

At this he became relaxed for the first time in many days. This eased state was so welcome that by comparison it told him just how tense he had been. He retrieved his shine-box from Frankie, who asked no questions. It was readily apparent that his young friend was feeling better, whatever the crisis had been, and he was glad he could be of help, whatever that may have meant. But he also was wise enough to know there was a shadow, and he couldn't help but continue to think there was some vague connection to Luigi Leopardi.

Business was good, and he would regularly go home with six or seven dollars, and sometimes more, a fair amount of money for a young boy to have in his pocket while walking on nearly empty streets late in the evening. His twelfth birthday had passed, as did the anniversary of his father's death. Spring came, as primitively welcome as it has always been since man first learned that the whims of nature governed his survival. The trees budded, there were birds and blue skies, and Americo began walking all the way home from Elmhurst one or two evenings a week.

These walks did not continue. Americo was earning a good income, and he was becoming more concerned about the dangers of being alone on dark streets. Ever since the night he followed Luigi and the woman he could not forget how easy it was, and how oblivious the couple had been to his presence. With so much money in his pocket he continued to worry about being followed, and how he could be overcome and robbed. He was getting well-known as the local shine-boy; his presence no longer entirely in the background anymore. Between his displays of growing skills and the obvious energy stoked by his concealed preoccupation with Luigi, the boy had surrendered his state of being barely visible and become an acknowledged part of the local scene, and everyone knew he had money in his pockets. The pleasure in the walk home wasn't worth the anxiety in the hour it took. Also, with looking back over his shoulder, straining to see if there was a figure or two in the shadows, his neck was getting sore. When taking a bus he could tell right away if he was being followed.

CHAPTER SIXTEEN

LUIGI NOTICED THE boy. While he didn't read every-thing hidden behind what he saw he had a sharp eye. He knew the boy worked hard, and he liked to see that in such a young person. He saw the boy made money, and he thought about some night taking his evening's pay from him. Luigi was a sport when it could make a nice show for his ego, but by nature he was a thief and a killer, and if money was in someone else's pocket he could not help but think of how a transfer could be affected. Still, he liked the boy, his attitude, the quality of his work, and a certain something that made him wonder if he was being reminded of himself as a youngster. He couldn't put his finger quite on it, and he kept watching him more than was apparent, one of his skills being that he could romance a woman, chat sweet flattery, look deeply into her eyes, and at the same time see pretty much everything that was going on in the room.

Every other week or so he asked the boy for a shine, and while he never gave him another five dollar bill he did give him a dollar, just to see that nice smile. America's best always beamed for Luigi. He was fascinated by America. Something about him pulled at his mind.

"Over here, shine. Let me have that good shine, boy."

"Yes sir, mister Luigi."

The man put his foot up on the box. America knelt on his pillow, and went to work. He was aware of the knife on his right hip, under his sweater, and whenever he shined his quarry's shoes he asked himself if this was the time. Working on the man's shoes he was ever watchful. It didn't matter that his eyes were directed at the shoe he was polishing, peripherally his focus was the entire man, calibrating the man's movements with the movements he had devised in his mind while practicing at home, the action he decided would give him success. From his watching he learned that there were, here and there, very short, rare moments when his wariness was distracted and his vital area exposed and available. These were moments of great hubris, when reacting to an exceptional bit of flattery his caution lapsed for just a flicker.

America never stopped practicing his draw-and-thrust at the mark on the wall at home, and by now the several parts of the act had become mentally and physically developed into that necessary one split-second motion, strong and accurate. He was so well rehearsed that when it finally happened it was emotionally rather plain, lacking the preliminary inner dramatics that repeatedly had led him to retreat from his resolve. America had made himself so ready that at precisely the most opportune moment the execution unfolded as if it were merely a naturally occurring act, like rain falling, or a breeze blowing. There were no introductory butterflies, no tremors of anticipation or fear. When the situation was right, there it was, in all its cause and effect simplicity.

A young, chubby but very pretty woman came to stand next to Luigi, and they talked.

"You comin' home with me, tonight, Marie?"

"Maybe you wanna talk to me and I can think it over, if it's somethin' I might find interestin' to do," and she paused coyly before saying, "or maybe not."

Luigi took a bill from his pocket and motioned for the bartender to give Marie whatever she wanted.

The woman smiled.

"Honey, I could make you scream for your momma."

"Maybe you could. I haven't had to do that for a long time." She drew out the word "long" with a languorous, do-it-to-me smile.

Luigi was pleased with himself, and, with his elbows back on the bar, he tilted his head backward and laughed from deep in his throat. As he laughed Americo saw this was the time. In that instant, without thinking, with no emotional surge, in one silky-smooth motion, he grasped his knife and thrust it between Luigi's ribs, into his black, animal heart.

For what seemed a long moment the room froze. Only Luigi's head moved, as he shifted his focus from the ceiling, (toward which he had been laughing,) to the knife handle sticking out from his chest. Americo leaned forward and grasped the man's left pinkie, put it into his mouth, sucked the ring from his finger, and swallowed it. Luigi stared at the boy and tried to hold on to the bar, to hold his weight up as he began to slide slowly to the floor. In shock, Luigi couldn't think of anything but that he was dying. The feared Luigi Leopardi killed in a bar, at the hand of a shoe-shine boy who had vaguely fascinated him. Who had taken that little ring with the stupid inscription, "Amore, Philomena."

As he struggled to remain upright he began sliding to the floor; for one long moment their heads were level. Eye to eye the two killers glared hatred at each other, and Americo whispered, "Amore, Philomena," the last words Luigi ever heard.

When his mortal enemy at last lay dead on the floor the room broke into a hubbub of activity. Amid the shouting and gasping the boy calmly sat down on his shine box, facing the room, his eyes staring at nothing. No one came near either him or the corpse. Although everyone was standing and excitedly talking, milling around in all the corners of the room, they left a large, empty semi-circle around the cause of this commotion. Crime was not unknown among these people, but this was murder.

The commotion was huge, with people talking fast and loud. There were a few shouts, the juke box was turned off, (someone pulled the plug,) and the police had been called. From a distance people began speaking to Americo, trying to get his attention but not approaching. Some even seemed to be pleading with him. He was impervious to their presence. His murdered father's ring was in his stomach, and the murderer was dead on the floor beside him. In this room filled with pandemonium he felt a peacefulness that he had longed for, and he was content to wait for what would happen to him. One thing was sure: he was about to enter the "system."

Chapter Seventeen

THE ABRUPT SHOCK of the sudden, explosive event was being talked about over and over in a jumble of many conversations. The crowding together people spoke to each other with a confusion of thoughts as they groped to find meaning in this baffling drama. Sooner than one might have expected the frightened, startled hubbub became subdued. Little by little a hint of jubilation crept in, and the mood in the room gradually began to brighten. A fearful monster had been slain, and that this had been done by a boy was the beginning of a local legend, destined to be remembered for decades as a proud part of the neighborhood's history. Calmer, the crowd was now just standing around, talking more reasonably about what they could hardly believe they had seen when two detectives pushed their way in and ordered everyone to get back against the walls farthest from the crime. Looking over the scene, one of them prodded the boy. There was no response. Sitting on his shine-box the boy was impassive, his arms folded on his lap.

"You do this, kid?"

Americo gave no recognition of being addressed.

"I'm detective McGinnis, my partner is detective O'Halloran. Did you do this?"

Again, no response. Americo was extremely serene, yet watchful. He was very much aware murder was a big event and he had no idea how he would be dealt with. He wanted to get a better grasp of what was happening, of what he faced.

The detective reached under the boy's arms and lifted him to a standing position, and moved him away from the body. Without his box the boy sat on the floor.

Mcginnis looked at the body. "Better call for the meat wagon," he told O'Halloran.

O'Halloran went to the bar and asked for the phone be-hind the bar-top. Before he dialed he said to his partner, "They say the shine kid did this. You better cuff him and then we'll take statements."

"Yeah. Okay." Going to Americo he bent over, rather than having to pick him up again, and handcuffed the boy's hands behind his back.

"We'll deal with you later, kid."

The two detectives busied themselves taking statements, pulling people from the crowd one at a time, off to the side, to record their words of what they had seen, along with their names and addresses. The stories were mostly all the same. There wasn't much to tell. The boy stabbed the man. There had been no argument, no awareness of bad blood between them, no provocation anyone could tell about, and no warning this was coming. There was laughter, and then there was death.

Soon after the detectives arrived two patrolmen appeared and stationed themselves outside the door to the street, to keep the gathering crowd from coming inside. A police photographer came and took some pictures. McGinnis, using a tissue, pulled the knife from Luigi's chest and placed it in a small paper bag. An ambulance showed up from which two men wearing white uniforms emerged, carrying a stretcher. They came in and took the body away. There was no blood on the floor, nothing to clean up. The event was about to become an indelible part of local history.

Americo watched and listened. He didn't know what was coming, only that he was in the "system" now, and it was going to chew him up. He wanted to stay alert and make note of everything, perhaps gaining some knowledge that would help him cope with his circumstances.

"Okay, kid, let's go." Mcginnis motioned for the boy to get up. O'Halloran picked up the shine-box. They walked out to their unmarked car and helped the handcuffed boy into the back seat. O'Halloran climbed in and sat beside him for the ride to the station-house. Through the car window Americo saw Frankie looking at him. They exchanged a glance of friendship, and the boy gave an abbreviated nod of salutation that was just barely perceptible. Frankie returned the nod with similar subtlety, worried for his friend.

"What's your name, kid?"

Americo didn't answer.

"Hey, talk to me. What's your name?"

Again silence.

O'Halloran, with a sudden violent swing, smacked the

boy across the side of his head, knocking him against the pad-
ded inside of the car door, dazing him momentarily. It was an
open-handed blow made with the back of a large, meaty hand.

"Kid, your name. Give." Before waiting for an answer he
smacked the boy again, hard. Again he was knocked against
the door.

"McGinnis, we got ourselves a hard case," and he gave
his obstinate adversary, the twelve year old boy in handcuffs, a
small, unconcerned, grimace.

Except for the night of his father's murder Americo had
never been struck, by anyone, ever. His father had never felt the
need to discipline him, and in the small circle of his narrow life
he had never met anyone who was familiar with violence. These
were the police and he knew they worked in a violent world. He
tried to think further about them and what he might expect,
given this introduction, but he was dizzy from the hard blows.

He also had never been in a car before and in the con-
fined space the cigarette smoke made his stomach queasy. He
knew his freedom was irrevocably gone and that possibly his
life was over too. The ride wasn't long. The two detectives
smoked and said nothing. When they arrived at the station
house they brought the boy inside and took his belt, his shoe
laces, his house key and his money, four and a half dollars,
an amount that surprised them. Never having had a wallet, or
having been issued any papers of identification, like a driver's
license or a social security card, there was nothing to be found
on his person with information. He was issued a John Doe receipt for his property, and placed in a holding cell, without cell
mates. This done they went to their separate desks where each
wrote a report on what they found at the crime scene, and then

they went to the captain's office to determine what should be done with the boy.

He was too young to be booked as an adult, but before turning him over to Juvenile they wanted the captain to be informed, and to make a judgment on exactly what it was they were going to do. They learned long ago not to make too many non-investigative decisions on their own: the captain, a complicated man with political hopes, often saw things from a different slant. Thoughtful and self-protective, he told them to hold off on Juvenile, insisting the detectives find out who he is and why he did this. He wanted a reason, and he wanted identification, period. His end of the case had to be documented. There would be no tolerance for work that could reflect poorly on his command. Luigi Leopardi was a known hardened criminal, and for several months there had been an on-going investigation into his recent activities. When the captain told them what to do, it was implicit he would accept no excuses for not following his orders and obtaining the results he demanded.

It was late, their shift was over, and they prepared to leave for the night.

"We'll start with the kid in the morning."

"Christ, he killed a guy! Just like that! Stuck him like a potato. You think they'll give him time in some kiddy pen?"

"We do our stuff. That other crap ain't our concern."

"It's on my mind."

"Don't think about it too much."

"I suppose tomorrow will be soon enough."

"See you in the a.m."

"Yeah. A day shift after an evening shift. Just for me."

"No. I'll be here, too."

"You wanna give the kid breakfast or go at him hungry."

"We'll look at him and then decide."

"I hope he don't give it up too easily."

"This one is different from the others."

"Luigi was a snake. Imagine a kid taking him like that."

"That's one reason I think this is gonna be different."

"What else?"

"I don't know, but I think we should use our heads a little."

"My head wants a skirt."

"Good night, O'Halloran."

CHAPTER EIGHTEEN

AMERICO WAS NOT only in a cell by himself, his cell was also away from the ones that held other criminals. He was alone, with no one around. There was a bed with a blanket, a sink with a half-used bar of soap, a damp towel, and a toilet. It was a small space, six by eight feet, with a steel barred window too high up for him to be able to look at the street. After stepping out of his lace less shoes he lay down, anticipating many restless hours in which to reflect on the day's two huge events: avenging his father's murder, and his arrest. When he put his head down his first thought in the silent darkness was, "I did it. I really did it!" With a sense of pride he found it pleasingly hard to believe that he had measured up to his own expectations of himself. Around his plan always hovered the self-questioning knowledge that he was only a boy day-dreaming of a glorious triumph. "Yes," he continued to himself, "I am a man just as I dared to hope I would be." When the moment of truth came he had stood tall. He had done it!

He pulled the blanket around his body, hugging himself for warmth. Even though he was in a jail cell, being alone seemed a great luxury after the day's extreme experiences, and overcome with an engulfing sense of satisfaction and pride he snuggled into the warmth his body was creating under the coarse blanket. Soon he closed his eyes, softly said one word, "Poppa," and fell into a deep sleep.

He awoke early in the morning with some stomach discomfort and immediately thought of his father's ring which he had swallowed. As cool as he may have seemed during the killing, that dramatic event and his arrest did affect his digestion. The result was a fortunately mild occurrence of diarrhea. Before flushing the toilet he put his hand into the bowl and searched for the ring. Then he flushed the toilet and brought his treasure to the sink where he rinsed it carefully, before swallowing it again. He had read about this ploy in a war story, and he smiled to himself about the advantages of an informal education.

Whatever might happen he felt he had to keep alert, he had to listen and observe and be cautious about what he revealed.

McGinnis and O'Halloran came for him soon after eight a.m. They were unsure about any guide lines or precedent concerning a twelve year old in police custody after a deliberate homicide. They had strong orders, and they went in thinking maybe the kid would soften his attitude after a night alone in a cell. If not they were going to have to invent a new procedure as they went along. Americo was a stubborn surprise, and almost immediately their intelligent intentions dissolved and they fell into the routines they had developed with hardened criminals.

They took him to an interrogation room where there were three wooden straight back chairs and an oak table stained with ink and coffee cup rings. On the floor there was an ominous large dark stain that might have been from old dried blood. There were odors of disinfectant and cigarette smoke.

"Okay, kid, it's a new day and we're starting out fresh. We didn't do so good last night, so let's get off to a better start today. First off, what's your name?"

Americo stared at the table, not making eye contact and in no way acknowledging they were even there. Being unsure of what would be best for him to do, he did and said nothing.

"Kid, let's do this easy. You must be hungry. Give us a story. You'll get breakfast, the captain will be happy. We'll all be happy."

McGinnis was talking. He sat on one long side of the table, opposite from the boy. At the short side, to Americo's left, sat O'Halloran. Neither detective took their eyes from the boy. They studied him carefully, looking for some reaction, some behavioral marker that would give them an indication about how to reach him.

"Listen, kid, I'm McGinnis, he's O'Halloran. You're not under arrest, you're in custody. You're a kid. You're going to Juvenile. But we can't give you to them without a story."

"It's the captain's orders," said O'Halloran, "we need a story."

Americo stared at the table. He had no thoughts regarding his situation and was lost in apprehension for this strange part of the world. What had been for him his usually reliable insight was no longer of use and the thought of trusting these men was out of the question. He had only trusted his father, and with his death responsibility for knowledge of his life lay with him alone.

"We need to start with your name. What's your name?"

Americo kept staring, and without warning O'Halloran, with the back of his very large, open hand smacked the boy across the side of his head, hard, much as he had in the car. The unexpected blow sent him crashing to the floor. He lay there, dazed for a moment, and then he got up, put his overturned chair upright, dusted his clothes and sat back in his place, staring at the table. What should he do?

O'Halloran leaned toward him. "You little wop bastard, you'll talk or I'll break your head open. What's your name?" The boy stared at the table and O'Halloran hit him again. Again the blow knocked him to the floor, overturning his chair, and again he got up, this time wobbly and dizzy, straightened the chair, dusted his clothes off, and resumed sitting and staring.

The two detectives looked at each other, then back at the boy.

McGinnis said, "Maybe the boy needs some breakfast."

"He gets crap until I get a name."

McGinnis felt there was a story here, and he wanted to hear it and move on. O'Halloran wanted to make his captain happy. Nothing more, nothing less.

They went on like this until noon, asking the same questions, receiving no answers, and not even a glance from the boy. O'Halloran, a big, fortyish man, whose face easily turned pink when he exerted himself, smacked him down maybe eight or ten more times.

"What'll it be, kid?" asked McGinnis. "You had no breakfast, and now it's lunchtime. How long are you going to keep this up? You must be hungry. Your stomach is going to hurt. We'll get the story eventually. Give it up, kid."

O'Halloran went to knock him to the floor again when the other man reached out to stop him. "Enough of that, O'Halloran. That's not getting us anywhere."

McGinnis was nearer to fifty, more slightly built, with black bushy eyebrows that lowered when he was in thought, somewhat shielding his eyes, as if preventing anyone from seeing his thoughts.

"Oh, yeah? Let's see how many days he can take this. It's not hurting me any."

They were silent for a while. Then O'Halloran spoke up. "Listen, kid, you're going to Juvenile. There's no serious hard time ahead for you. What's the problem? What's the point? You're a goddamn wop kid. You killed and you're goin' to a kids' joint until you're eighteen, and then you'll go out and kill again. Then we'll get you and fry you good. And it will never matter what your damn name was."

This explanation made Americo furious. Furious! He was proud of himself, enormously proud of having endured a relentless parade of emotional hardships and physical challenges. And he had become proud of his cleverness at staying away from the scrutiny of the system; his navigation through the daily tests of a lonely, determined life, dedicated to obeying his father's dying wish. "Stay out of the system, Americo. Stay out of the system."

The only purpose of his struggle was to grow into manhood and take a place in society, to become of age and no longer

109

have to keep the secrecy of his life. He hadn't counted on meeting his father's murderer. Nor how such a meeting would undo the distance that time and healing had mercifully begun to generate between his pain and the constant attention demanded of him just for daily survival. And he hadn't counted on how the depth of his love for his father, combined with the echoes of his father's words about pride and honor, spoken to him so often, how these feelings and memories would rise again to the surface of his consciousness, urging him, and eventually compelling him, to avenge the terrible and hauntingly painful thing that had been done.

But now Americo couldn't keep silent anymore and without warning he exploded, startling the two men.

"I'm not a kid! I'm a man!" He banged the table with both his fists as he shouted through clenched teeth, his saliva bursting forth with his words through the small spaces between his teeth, some spraying the air, some accumulating on his chin. His chest was heaving with large breaths of air, his eyes glaring with all the raging strength of his soul, and further fueled with the aching pain of his loss and his loneliness.

"I'm a man! I'm a man!" He banged on the table, loud and hard, several more times "I'm a man! I'm a man!"

The men were startled by the vehemence of the boy's first words. They looked searchingly at him.

"You're just a kid, that's all I see. A kid that killed someone."

"I'm a man!" He hit the table again.

O'Halloran snorted. "You're a dumb wop kid."

"I'm a man! I'm a man! I'm a man!" Now his shouting came from deep in his chest like the roaring of a lion. "I avenged my father's murder."

They looked at him carefully.

"I am America, and I did justice!" He shouted more loudly, from deeper within his chest, and passionately banged his fists on the table four more times.

The three of them sat there in silence, the men pondering the boy's words, the boy heaving as he took deep gasps of breath, fighting back tears of anger, sadness and hunger.

CHAPTER NINETEEN

THE TWO DETECTIVES remained quiet, eying the boy for any glimpse of some familiar body language, something they could equate with an entry in their dictionary of tell-tale signs. They were intimate with a countless host of body movements and verbal and facial expressions that betrayed manipulation, lying, and clever misdirection. They possessed a mental compilation of signs accumulated through years of questioning suspects in the lower end of human distress. They were looking for one sign that would enable them to translate the boy's plain-spoken words into the language of their familiar commerce with liars, cheats, thieves and killers.

McGinnis sensed O'Halloran was about to smack the boy again, and again he reached over and touched his arm. He felt there was something genuine about this boy, and if he could communicate this then the boy might perceive him as a positive presence, and open up. "Tell us about your father."

Other than in the needs of domestic trade, with the store owners in his small part of Corona, and with his landlord, Americo had never told anyone a word about his father, about his life or his death. The detectives couldn't know if there was family or not. None of the crime witnesses they had interviewed knew anything about the boy. Almost none of them knew him by any other name but Shine. Nothing about where he was from, what neighborhood, what school. Nothing.

"Go on, kid, you want to tell us. We know you want to, and that's okay. We'll listen to your story."

Americo had kept his secret, but his success did not lessen the fact that it was a burden to him. He did want to talk about it. He was surely in the system now, and it was becoming clear to him his situation was not going to change, regardless of what he did or did not say. He felt McGinnis recognized him as a person, which was in part true and in part owing to the detective's skill as an interrogator.

The difficult truth which he had carefully avoided thinking was that his big secret had engendered many small secrets, and the constellation of these secrets weighed on him. They weighed on him and weighed on him, day after day after day, more than he thought about. In this respect his loneliness was total and relentless. Yes, in a strangely compatible duality, the blitheness of his character often rose above these burdens, and the tenor of his life was not depressive, even with the underlying awareness that if he dared to drop his guard for just a moment it would likely be the end of his freedom, the end of being able to control his own life, and to make his own decisions. It would be the end of the proud enjoyment of his daily inventions in living by his wits, and of the serious game of expanding the range and ability of his cleverness. And, worst of all, it would be the end of the joy he found in eating food earned by his own sweat and skill.

Now all that was over. Maybe by talking he could be relieved of his life's subtext, that tension of secrecy. He was in the system, irretrievably so. He was resigned, and he saw he could give up that part of his struggle, and, who knows, perhaps what he saw as the truth and honor of his story would earn for him at least an adversarial respect from these large men of the law.

"There were two of them." And Americo described the events of that mortal encounter.

"When did this happen?"

"It was in the evening. I told you."

"No, kid, the date."

Americo told them. He could never forget it.

"Maybe you heard about a killing and you're just making it a part of your big phony story," commented O'Halloran, looking for a reaction.

"You're smart enough," added McGinnis.

"No. It's all true." The boy was calm now.

"We'll check with the morgue. The medical examiner will have a record of this Giovanni fellah."

"No. They took my father's wallet and ring. He had nothing else. Nothing with a name. What about the ring? My father's ring."

"Is that what you were doing? The witnesses said you did something with Luigi's hand as he was dying."

"Yes. I sucked the ring from his finger. It had my mother's name inside." After a pause he added, "That's how Luigi got the ring, he spit on my poppa's finger." His voice was rising again. "That man, he stabbed my poppa in the back, and then he spit on his finger!"

"What did you do with it?"

"I swallowed it."

"And it didn't go down the sewer this morning, did it?"

"No. I cleaned it and swallowed it again."

The men thought for a moment. After some silent minutes O'Halloran asked, "Maybe you killed him for the ring."

"Yeah. You saw the ring. You liked it, and you plotted to go for it."

"A savage would kill for a shiny piece of glass!"

"Yes, I wanted the ring." Americo's voice was rising. "But I killed him for justice!"

He was breathing harder and they could see he was getting agitated. McGinnis distracted the trend of their conversation, saying, "This is all good. We've made real progress. Let's break for some food."

"Yeah. Okay," added O'Halloran. "I'm hungry, too."

"Whaddya want, kid?"

They settled on a couple of salami sandwiches and a soda for the very hungry Americo. O'Halloran would decide what he would get for himself at the little deli across the street. McGinnis' wife had packed him his lunch so he was going to stay with the boy.

As O'Halloran left McGinnis turned to the boy and asked, "Want a cup of coffee while we're waiting?"

"Tea?"

"Coffee's it, kid. We can put a little cream and sugar in it."

At the mention of sugar the boy brightened. "With cream and sugar."

"How many sugars?"

"Six."

McGinnis smiled. "I'll bring the sugar. You put it in yourself."

McGinnis was pleased. They had secured some easing of the boy's guard, and it hadn't taken as long as he feared it could. Having had a little light banter he was sure they would get the story. And his sixth sense told him there might also be some money somewhere in this. This kid had been through some strange and extremely difficult times, and, as far as he could see, had survived on his own. He was beginning to appreciate how very smart and direct the boy's thinking was, and that he was plenty tough, although it was apparent he also had a certain softness, and that in his young mind there wasn't the slightest hint of a real criminal's hardness.

Mcginnis left and in a moment returned with two cups of coffee, one black, for himself, and one light, which he put in front of the boy. Then he left the room and quickly returned with the sugar and a spoon. He watched as the boy put six spoonfuls of sugar into the hot coffee, and he smiled again as the boy then began blowing on the hot coffee, and sipping. And then more quickly blowing and sipping, blowing and sipping.

"You have a real sweet tooth, don't you?"

The boy nodded, and kept blowing and sipping, blowing and sipping, until it was gone. Then he asked for another cup, and McGinnis smiled as he left to get it for him.

O'Halloran came in with the sandwiches. They ate, using the sandwich wrapping papers for plates. The detectives had black coffee and Americo was now drinking soda. They ate without talking.

Having eaten, and a dialogue having begun, they all felt better, a little more relaxed, but the detectives, being veterans, were inwardly as wary as ever. McGinnis' interest was heightened by the revelations of the morning; even O'Halloran was getting curious.

"We need more details, more information."

"There's not enough here to make a story we can bring to the captain," said O'Halloran.

"What else is there to tell?" asked Americo.

"Assuming there was a dead man found that night, we need some proof that it was your father. Some evidence, some identifying mark."

"Did he see a dentist?" asked O'Halloran.

"He never said he did."

"We need something, kid."

"We can't go to the morgue with nothing but a date."

They sat quietly for a while.

"He had a two dollar bill in his shoe."

Again the detectives studied the boy, weighing his words against the expression on his face as he offered the information.

"They didn't get that," continued Americo.

"That's good, but, you know, a lot of people have a two dollar bill."

"For luck."

"You got a two dollar bill, McGinnis?"

"I do."

"I got one, too."

"But it was in his shoe!"

"If the guy in the morgue found it he would keep it. He wouldn't log it in. He wouldn't admit he ever saw it."

"Sorry, kid. I believe you. But it's not a story I can bring to the captain."

"Think of something else."

"Relax. Something'll come to you."

They sat for another while.

"I remember the serial number."

The detectives leaned forward, their interest piqued by this odd revelation, studying this strange boy ever more carefully.

"That might be something."

O'Halloran put a pad and pencil on the table.

"Write it down."

Americo wrote the number. 12577521.

"Why do you remember it?"

"It's the same backward and forward. My father said it was special."

The two men studied the number.

"What do you want to do?" asked O'Halloran, talking to McGinnis.

"That creepy kraut, what's his name, Kahn; he's still down at the morgue, ain't he?"

"Yeah. I seen him there a couple of weeks ago."

"Gimme that number." He took the pad and removed the sheet on which the boy had written. "I got an idea. Keep the kid here. Get him some coffee. God, he likes it sweet. I'll be back soon." He left, his spirits lifted at the prospect of playing a little cat and mouse with the unsuspecting Kahn.

CHAPTER TWENTY

THEY SAT AND drank coffee. It wasn't as hot as before, when it was freshly made. O'Halloran looked at the boy with interest.

"How old are you."

"Twelve."

"Any family?"

"No."

"Just you and your father."

"Yes." Americo swayed a bit in his chair.

"You okay?"

"A little dizzy."

O'Halloran continued looking at him without commenting.

"You hit me pretty good."

"I like hitting. If you hadn't opened up I would have kept at it."

"Why?" He put the question uncomplainingly, in a flat, matter-of-fact tone.

"I told you, kid, I like it."

Americo looked at his face, the features broad and faintly battle scarred.

"Don't wait for an apology. I was havin' a good time."

The longer the boy was here the more deeply he grasped this world was very different from anything he could comprehend, nor could he possibly devise a better way to navigate through the routines and regulations.

The door opened and a uniformed policeman motioned to O'Halloran to come to the door, where he whispered in his ear.

The policeman left and O'Halloran closed the door.

"There's a nigra here to see you."

Americo could see that O'Halloran was suspicious of his being visited by a black man.

"That must be Frankie."

O'Halloran eyed the boy with some irritation.

"Why'd he come to see you?"

"He's a friend. We're friends."

After a wait O'Halloran said, "I'll take you where you two can visit."

Americo got up and O'Halloran escorted him down a hall, to a small room with two chairs facing each other across a small table. "Take a seat. I'll bring him in."

He went out and in a minute he came back with Frankie. The boy made a small smile as Frankie sat down at the table. When O'Halloran went to the door to leave the room he turned and said, "You got five minutes," then he shut the door behind him.

"Hello, Shine."

"Hello, Big Frank," then he added, "It's nice to see you. Thanks."

They sat, the two friends glad to see each other again.

"You got some big trouble."

"I'll be okay."

"It's going to be a long time before the people down there stop talking about you."

"Yeah." After a moment of silence he added, "You don't look surprised."

"You can't surprise me, Shine. I know almost nothin' about you, but since we met I made you for a deep shadow. There's always a lot goin' on in that head of yours."

"I guess."

"It never rests with you, boy. Always carrying a big load. Only now you look like it's a lot lighter."

"I killed the man who murdered my poppa."

Frankie nodded.

They sat quietly, not saying anything. Americo had his hands folded together on the table before him. After some minutes Frankie reached out and put his large brown hand on the boy's two hands.

"I have to go now. If there's anything you need here's my phone number." He brought a small piece of paper from his shirt pocket. "Anything. Nobody else has this number. Learn it," and he showed the boy the paper without handing it to him.

He studied the paper for a moment. "Thanks, Big Frank."

"Maybe sometime you'll call to say hello."

He rose and stepped to the door. When he opened it O'Halloran appeared; as the detective entered he pointed down the hall, to where Frankie should leave. He motioned for the boy to come with him, and they returned to the interrogation room.

They sat down, in the same chairs as before.

"He's your friend, huh?"

Yeah. He taught me how to be a real shine-boy. He knows a lot of stuff."

"I'll bet he does."

At that moment McGinnis walked in, with a broad smile.

Going closer he leaned over and placed a two dollar bill on the table, between the boy and O'Halloran. It bore the serial number the boy had written for them, and it still had the crease marks where Giovanni had originally folded it.

"Jesus, Mary, Joseph!" whispered O'Halloran.

Americo stared at the bill.

"What do you think, kid?" asked McGinnis.

Americo looked up at the detective. As tears appeared he wiped his eyes with his hands and fought them back. There it was. His father's spirit seemed to be in the room, giving him approval, and from the grave testifying to his truthfulness. It was a while before he could stop crying.

The two large men looked sadly at the boy and with some measure of respect wondered at the simple truth of his complicated story.

"How'd you do it, Mac?"

"Easy. I love it when these guys don't know I have them cold. I got all the cards and they play like they're winners."

O'Halloran smiled, anticipating the small tale of the unmasking of Kahn.

"I go in there pretending I wanted to talk about that

stiff we worked on last week. I asked Kahn some patty-cake questions, and he's filling me in like he's some professor with a dope. Then we had some coffee and started talking. Pretty soon he asked about you, and I told him about your getting a two dollar bill from a guy someplace, and you were so proud yours had a serial number with five twos, and I showed him mine with five sevens. And we laughed, and he had to show me one he had where the numbers were the same backward and forward."

"Nice."

"Listen to this. While he's holding the deuce for me to see the serial I take out the paper with the numbers the kid wrote, and when I show it to him I tell him how he's going to lose his pension and go to stir for robbing dead bodies."

"What did he say?"

"Nothin.' He looked like one of his customers."

Americo was bewildered.

"I told him the date he took the bill, and he said that was probably right. Then I took the bill and told him when I wrote my report I would do what I could to keep him on the job."

"You didn't!"

"He owes me. Large."

CHAPTER TWENTY-ONE

"Your story's okay. A few details and we'll take you to Juvenile," McGinnis said, with the more easy-going demeanor of interest and respect.

"I didn't think you'd check out," said O'Halloran.

"Tell me, kid, you planned this pretty good. Maybe for a long time?" asked McGinnis.

"No. I didn't look for him. I never thought to look for him, that I could find him. It had been many months. I just by accident found him. One night he was there." Americo swayed a little in his chair.

"You all right, kid?" asked McGinnis.

"I'm all right."

What about the other guy?" asked O'Halloran.

"What other guy?"

"Didn't you say there were two of them?"

"Oh, yeah. I never think about him. I never saw his face. It was night, dark. Luigi stepped into some light and we looked at each other. He knew I saw him, but there were police coming."

"So you were shining shoes a long time before you saw him," said McGinnis, returning the conversation to its original line.

"I knew him right away. I could never forget him." He stared into space as he recalled that awful night, his expression wistful and hurt.

"So that was when you started thinking about killing him."

"It was justice. Don't you believe in justice? He killed my poppa!" He was getting agitated again. "He killed him! He stopped his life!"

"Take it easy, kid. We only want to know what you can tell us."

"Where'd you get the knife? From the nigra?" prodded O'Halloran.

"No! Nobody knew anything. I talked to nobody. Not a word."

"The knife. Where'd you get it?"

"The Army-Navy over on Roosevelt."

"You got a receipt?" asked O'Halloran.

"I might. It might be at home."

"Where's home?"

He told them the address.

"You live there alone, since your father died?"

"Yes."

"All these months, over a year, alone?"

"Yes."

"And all this time you kept your secret."

"Nobody knew anything about you."

"That's right."

McGinnis stood up. "Let's go look at your home."

They went to Property and asked for Americo's house key. O'Halloran handcuffed the boy and they went to their car, and drove to the address Americo had given them.

They drove without talking until they were on his street.

"It's the middle of the next block. On the left."

McGinnis slowed the car down.

"There. Between the gray house and the one with the fake brick siding."

"There's nothing there, kid."

"You'll see. Park in front of the hedge."

Mcginnis parked the car.

"Here?"

"Here."

The men got out first, then helped the handcuffed Americo get out. They walked on either side of him, until he gestured with his shoulder to an opening in the hedge.

"Through there."

They had to go through the opening one at a time, McGinnis first, then the boy, and then O'Halloran. One of the old women in the neighborhood saw them, and, seeing Americo in handcuffs, she went to the grocery store to tell Mrs. Quattrocci.

They walked on the path alongside Mr. Inzerillo's house until they came to the little peculiar structure where Americo had lived. McGinnis unlocked the door and the three of them entered. It was still light outside but inside the light was dim. O'Halloran found the lamp and turned it on; the soft snap of the switch was loud in the silence.

They looked around without touching anything.

"It looks pretty clean. Everything neat," said O'Halloran.

They looked at the tiny toilet, the sink, the half-size refrigerator, the hot plate.

"I cleaned carefully. Twice a week. My poppa taught me."

"These weights yours?"

"Yes. I was alone and I wanted to be strong."

O'Halloran pointed to the scar on the wall around a black mark, where Americo had practiced how he would kill Luigi. "What are these marks?"

"That's where I practiced." He paused. "How to attack Luigi. I couldn't make a mistake or he would kill me."

"Practiced?"

"I put my box on the floor, there, just under it, and pretended to be shining a shoe, and wearing the knife under my sweater. I practiced taking the knife and stabbing the mark, quick, smooth, into Luigi's heart."

The three of them stood quietly. The detectives looked at the boy, and they looked at each other. He had spoken so simply of so enormous a thing to do. A boy revenging himself on a crime-hardened career criminal, it was incomprehensible, impossible, yet here it was. McGinnis and O'Halloran took out their notepads and wrote for several minutes.

Americo looked around the room with disappointment. With the two detectives there he felt his father's spirit had left the room. It had transformed from a place filled with the memories of a young lifetime into just a place where he used to live.

It was hard for them to take the measure of America's character. They thought back through the years of their experience and there weren't any comparisons to be made. This boy was unique. If they went by the book they would be on safe ground, at least regarding the captain, but they were becoming less and less sure how they really should treat the boy. It was getting difficult not to admire his easy independence, his remarkable straightforwardness, and his intensity. When this was over America would be taken to some institution to live, but what would it be like? How would he live there, and did it matter?

"That radio work?" asked McGinnis.

"Yes. I don't play it much. My poppa listened to news. The war."

"You and your father lived here?" asked O'Halloran.

"Yes."

"And he was very secretive about the two of you here."

America nodded his head. "He said if the wrong people knew about us I would be taken away to an institution, a home."

"He was right about that."

O'Halloran pointed to a small neat stack of books on the table.

"They're from the library. I have to return them."

"You read a lot?"

"Every day, until three, when school is out and a boy can be expected to be seen on the streets, without someone asking questions." He explained his father's strategy to keep his presence from causing any inquiries.

McGinnis walked back to the door and bent over, picking up a letter addressed to Giovanni. He didn't have to open it to see it was a government check.

"Your father still gets mail?"

Americo reddened.

"You been cashing these checks, kid?"

"Yes."

"That's forgery. We're talking federal."

"I know it's wrong. I had to."

"Yeah. You had to." Mcginnis wrote "deceased" on the envelope and said, "We'll drop this in a mail box on the way back." Looking at O'Halloran he added, "And we won't mention this again."

"Thank you."

"You get heat from the house this is attached to?" asked O'Halloran.

"Yes."

"He the landlord?" He pointed to the other side of the wall.

"Mr. Inzerillo."

"We'll give him the key when we leave."

"Take a last look around, Americo," said O'Halloran. You won't be seeing this place again no more."

"Is there anything here you want to take with you? Anything that means something special to you. They can hold it in Property until you get out."

Americo was hesitant.

"What is it, kid?" asked McGinnis.

"My money," he whispered.

"Money," repeated McGinnis. And then he said, "I wondered when we would get to that."

"Where?" asked O'Halloran.

"In the corner. There's a piece of floor you can pick up if you're careful."

O'Halloran walked over and after a little wriggling he lifted the piece of flooring, put his hand into the opening, and withdrew the tin box. McGinnis took the box from O'Halloran and opened it. He let out a low whistle as he picked up the sheaf of bills that was held together by a rubber band.

"You live here alone, you work hard, you're careful. You got a nice little bundle, kid," said O'Halloran admiringly. "How much is there," he asked Mcginnis, who was busy counting.

"Two hundred forty five."

Americo walked over to the armchair and sat down, uncertainly.

"You all right?" asked McGinnis.

"I'm fine."

"He seemed a little shaky a couple times, but then right away he's okay."

"He's all right, ain't you, kid?"

"Yeah."

"You'd say something if you wasn't, yes?"

"I feel fine."

McGinnis counted out one hundred and twenty dollars and handed that to O'Halloran. As O'Halloran took the money McGinnis said, "I'll keep the odd fin." It was the equivalent of a month's pay for each of them.

"That's mine!" exclaimed Americo.

"Listen, sonny, where you're going you won't need any money for at least six years," answered O'Halloran.

"Show a little gratitude, kid. We're cutting you a lot of

slack. There's no way you can have this. Not where you're going. Either we take it for ourselves now or someone you don't know takes it from Property while you're wherever Juvenile sends you." As he said this McGinnis assumed a stern, intense stare and bent to look Americo directly in the eye. "We can do you some good, capeesh?"

Americo was quiet, and then he nodded.

What could he accomplish if he persisted? He was in the system. This was the bargain he made for himself when he decided to step outside the law. And how much more varied and oppressive it could become he knew he was destined to find out. At this moment all he really wanted was to be out of these handcuffs, and out of that cell he would get returned to at night. He looked forward to Juvenile even though he had no idea what that was. He liked working and he knew that was over too, as well as eating in the diner, and visiting the library and running into Annette. He thought back to when he worried that she had been hit by a car.

Aside from the compulsive smacking around he got from O'Halloran when he was first taken into custody, he intermittently sensed from the two detectives, at unexpected times, a degree of compassion, and at others, only duty by the book. He could see that they had certain boundaries which they wouldn't cross for fear of trouble with their superior, the captain. They could do things that seemed criminal, like stealing his money, when there was little or no chance of their having to answer for their choices.

McGinnis reached into the box and removed the papers that were there, looked them over, and put them in his inside jacket pocket.

"Okay, first we give the key to the landlord and tell him the place is empty and he should do as he likes with what's here. And he better not rent it to anyone with kids or we'll come down hard."

"You know, Mac, I think the kid was good here."

Ignoring him McGinnis continued, "Then we drop these books at the library, pick up some sandwiches and get back to the station."

"Good. We can meal while writing our reports and go home without more overtime." "I've had enough of that for a while," added McGinnis.

"We got a lot to report, so let's move."

McGinnis led the way, Americo next, and then O'Halloran, with his hand on the boy's shoulder. As they emerged from the opening in the hedge a substantial crowd had gathered, waiting to see what was going on with their polite young neighbor with the nice smile. McGinnis stood with Americo, handed the key to O'Halloran, pointing for him to take it to the landlord.

Among the onlookers was Annette, who looked at Americo with wistful sorrow. He returned her gaze, his face revealing to her his equally poignant sadness. They were on the edge of adolescence and were strongly drawn to one another. They had dreamed of each other, but they would never see each other again. People were asking the detective what the boy had done. McGinnis ignored the group and ushered the boy into the back of the car. Everybody in the crowd looked shocked and concerned as O'Halloran returned to sit in the back seat. Americo was surprised there were so many of his neighbors gathered to view this scene. They weren't merely there for the spectacle of a young fellow in handcuffs. They had come to like this youngster and were concerned as well as curious. McGinnis drove as Americo leaned at the window for a last glimpse of Annette. They stopped at the library, and then got sandwiches.

When they arrived at the station they took Americo with them to their desks, removed his handcuffs, and gave him two of the sandwiches and a soda. O'Halloran went and got some coffee for himself and McGinnis, and they sat and ate, the two men typing from their notepads.

"Can I talk to you while you do that?"

"Sure."

"I want to keep my father's ring." This he said to McGinnis.

"That will be difficult. To do that means I'll have to keep it out of my report." He looked at his partner. "You hear that, O'Halloran?"

"We can do that for the kid."

"You'll have to hide it for six years or it's our pensions on the line." McGinnis overstated their risk to makes sure Americo viewed the favor as huge, and worth what he was paying for with his confiscated savings.

"I'm good with secrets."

"I guess you are, at that."

"And the two dollar bill?"

McGinnis thought for a moment, and then he said, "We can't leave that out. It's a key piece of the puzzle. We'll lay out the whole story for the captain. He'll see the sentimental importance of the bill. It will be up to him. He might go for it."

"Terrific piece of evidence," said O'Halloran

He reflected for a moment. "I can see how much that deuce means to you, and that makes plenty of sense. If we do it officially it will go to the head of whatever place you're sent to, and they'll hold it for you until your release." Then he added, "Why not do the same thing with the ring?"

"No! I want it with me. I want my poppa with me!"

"Okay, kid. But I want to see that ring in the morning. Clean it good."

CHAPTER TWENTY-TWO

THEIR REPORTS TOOK longer to write than they expected, and by the time they finished the captain had left for the day. They took the boy to the same cell he had been in, and they told him they would be coming for him about nine or nine thirty in the a.m., after they had time to go over their reports with the captain.

"The hard part's over, kid. We got what the captain wanted; now you'll go to Juvenile. He likes neat, and it's all here. Maybe later tomorrow, maybe the day after at the latest."

McGinnis was in his compassionate mode.

In a calm, unemotional tone O'Halloran interrupted, "Don't you ever forget, you murdered a man in cold blood. You're a killer. You planned it, you practiced it, and you did it. Whatever the reasons, or who will or will not find sympathy for you, that's what you did, and no reasons, no excuses can change the simple fact of what you did. You killed."

Americo hadn't had much of his dinner and McGinnis handed the wrapped up uneaten sandwiches to the boy to have later. They assumed his appetite was off after the finality of his last ever leave-taking from the comforting isolation of his home. Even they could feel the sense of sanctuary in the secrecy of that room, where loneliness was both painful and reassuring. Then McGinnis touched O'Halloran on the arm and they started to move away.

"Good night, Americo. Get a good night's sleep."

Since his arrest that was the first time he heard his name spoken.

His father had always called him Americo. Sometimes he used the diminutive Rico, but he never called him kid, or anything else. Now he was "kid," or referred to as "the boy." For how long does one get to be called kid, he wondered. Is it a question of height? Would he have to be tall? His father wasn't tall. Would he always be "kid?" Or was age part of it? What age? Sixteen? Eighteen? Twenty-one?

He hated being in the cell. It seemed to him Juvenile wouldn't have cells. Still, it was nice to be alone. Having been alone so much he found it soothing to be in his own company. He liked himself. He believed he had always been fair and honorable in every way he dealt with others. He excused his forgery as a necessity for survival, although he was beginning to doubt he should have continued it for so long. After all, he was accumulating money, lots of it. Now he had no money at all.

He reflected again on his killing of Luigi. "I am a man," he said to himself. "I did the manly thing. My poppa's soul can rest. He had a man for a son." He covered himself with the blanket, snuggled comfortably, and fell asleep, enjoying thinking of himself as a brave and respectable man.

The guard on the floor had little to do with Americo. He looked into his cell every hour or so, saw that he was asleep, and let him be. McGinnis left word with the unit sergeant, Buonaiuto, who was in charge of the guards who kept watch over the different cells, that they would be late the next morning. When he awoke, after a good, deep sleep, Americo got out of bed and washed. He drank some water from the tap, and then sat on the toilet. Having done his business he looked around to be sure he was not being observed, and reached into the bowl and retrieved his father's ring.

The guard, not the same one as the night before, brought him some toast and coffee, and six little packets of sugar, attending to the instructions had been left for that prisoner. Americo wasn't too hungry but he ate some of the toast. The sweet coffee was wonderful and he called the guard and asked for another cupful. The guard was amused to have such a young charge, and he was happy to get him more coffee and sugar.

"You're lucky, kid. The coffee is good today. Not always, I can tell you that."

McGinnis and O'Halloran came by at nine-thirty. The guard unlocked the door for them and McGinnis told the guard, "We're going into the cell with the kid for a few minutes. You can leave it open. When we leave we'll call you, and you can eye it over, just so you know everything's okay."

When they were alone O'Halloran said, "We need to see the ring here because when we go back we have to go straight to the captain."

"Let's see it," said McGinnis.

"We can't take your word for anything. We just need to see it," said O'Halloran.

With misgivings Americo took the ring from his pocket. The cell's light was not too bright and O'Halloran was prepared for that having brought a small, pencil shaped flashlight. He took the ring and shone the light on it.

"Not much of a ring, kid."

"It was a gift from my mother. She was a cleaning lady. It's the best ring in the world."

After a moment's study of the ring he replied, "Maybe it is, Americo. Maybe it is."

"Can you read what it says inside, Mac?" He handed the ring to McGinnis.

"Yeah. Amore, Philomena."

"You said I could keep it," said Americo, reaching his hand for the precious ring.

O'Halloran took the ring from McGinnis and gave it to the boy.

McGinnis said, "I don't know, kid. There must be a lot of rings like that. If it weren't for the inscription there might be a little problem here."

"The inscription makes it right, Mac. Let's go see the captain."

"Yeah. It all checks out." Then, turning to the boy, he said, "We don't have too many stories check out like this."

"I don't tell lies."

"Oh, right. You're forgery and murder."

"Let's go."

As they walked to the captain's office Americo was thinking over their conversation. He would never get the last word, and he should stop trying to tell them how he saw himself.

He was in the system, their system. In their measurements

he would never be himself. Let it go. They will define him the way they need to. He will never believe them, and they will never believe him, not in that way.

The captain was behind his desk, not so much sitting as reigning. One might think he was basking in a spotlight brightly shining in his imagination, a spotlight that beamed only for him, wherever he went, whatever he was doing. Ever meticulously groomed, his uniforms, shirts included, were expensively and flatteringly tailored, furthering his air of intimidation.

Entering his office Americo immediately understood why the detectives had to be so careful in the details of their investigations. They dared not incur this man's disappointment and anger. McGinnis and O'Halloran were caught in the system, too. Maybe the Irish didn't have fathers like Giovanni; he smiled to himself.

"I've read your reports. Very clean. Complete. Good work. Now he belongs to Juvenile.

And we're rid of Luigi."

"Who should we call over there, Captain?"

"Let's see. No, not Goldberg. He doesn't even like kids. How about Meskalik?"

"She's nice."

"Call her. What's her first name?"

"Arlene."

"Call her."

"Anything else, captain?"

"No. We're done here. You can keep an eye on what happens, but we're done."

The detectives got up. O'Halloran took the boy's shoulders and lifted him from the chair. Americo hadn't moved and probably wouldn't without prodding. The short interlude with Malloy had him mesmerized. The disdain, the pursing of the lips, his personal pretension, and he didn't even once look in his direction; to him it was nothing short of a performance. And he had never seen a performance until now.

They went back to their desk area and sat down.

"Now you've met the captain."

"You get the picture better now, kid?" asked O'Halloran.

Americo nodded his head in agreement.

Then O'Halloran said to McGinnis, "Call Juvenile."

"How about I call Jacobson?"

"No. The skirt."

"Meskalik?"

"That's what the captain said, call Meskalik."

McGinnis shrugged, picked up the phone and dialed.

The boy looked around the office while McGinnis explained the case to the lady in Juvenile. They talked for a long time, and then McGinnis put the phone down, and turned to Americo.

"They're very busy over there. A uniform is taking them copies of our reports. She'll be over after lunch to interview you."

O'Halloran interrupts, "A lot is up to her. Answer everything the best you can. The best thing you got going is be truthful. Your situation, this and leading up to this, that's what she has to consider in making a determination."

"What's that?"

"Which facility she recommends you spend the next six years at."

"It can make a difference, kid. A real difference."

Listening to this Americo was feeling more and more helpless. He was in the system only two days and he couldn't imagine coping with years of this. Fear and anger were growing within him. The anger he could handle, the fear they could see.

"You'll like her, kid. She has a knockout smile."

McGinnis looked at his watch. "They have lunch early. She said to expect her between twelve thirty and a quarter of."

After thinking for a minute O'Halloran said, "We're going to have to be around while she's in the interview room with him."

"Go for sandwiches a quarter to twelve," McGinnis answered. By the time you get back and we eat and clean up, we'll be ready for her."

Looking at Americo McGinnis asked, "You want me to take you back to the cell or sit here while we do paperwork?"

"Can I read the paper and drink coffee?"

McGinnis looked at O'Halloran. "Give the kid the paper; I'll get us coffee. You want some, too?"

O'Halloran nodded and reached over to get the paper from atop a filing cabinet.

Americo read about the war while McGinnis and O'Halloran smoked cigarettes and typed. Soon it was time for O'Halloran to get their lunch. Then they ate, the detectives still typing as they chewed their sandwiches and drank coffee. Americo's appetite was still off, which they attributed to his obvious nervousness at the up-coming interview. They had cleaned up and were on a second cup of coffee when Miss Meskalik appeared.

"Hello, detectives."

After they returned her greeting she looked at Americo.

"Is this the boy?" she asked, knowing, of course, that he was.

"Kid, stand up and say hello."

"Hello."

"We'll be okay. I know where the interview rooms are."

"Take the second one. We'll be right here if you have any questions."

"All right, young man, this way." And she led him to interrogation room number two.

She had him walk in front of her, with her hand lightly on his shoulder, guiding his way. When they reached the door she reached in front of him and opened it.

All the interrogation rooms were the same, a table and three chairs, a window with bars, gray painted walls, and the usual assortment of stains on the floor.

She indicated for him to sit on one side of the table and she sat on the other side, facing him. Until now her expression had been neutral, neither this nor that. She opened the folder with the reports, and looked up at the boy and smiled. Like O'Halloran had said, it was an amazing smile. Americo was momentarily disarmed, but quickly he reminded himself where he was and why; that he was in the system, and he should be careful. His mind was working, even as his heart was beating more quickly, and his skin was tingling.

He was still just barely adolescent, and the presence of an attractive woman was an event, a distraction from where his attention needed to be.

Chapter Twenty-Three

"Are you comfortable?"

"Yes, Miss."

"You must be an extremely brave young man, Americo."

"I don't know."

"You killed a very bad man."

"He murdered my poppa."

"Yes, that was born out by the evidence."

He looked at her flawless skin, creamy and smooth.

"Have you been in trouble before?"

"No, miss."

"Well, Americo, there's no record of your ever having been in trouble before. We know, however, that it is still a possibility that you have been. It will be better for you to tell me. I'm not here to punish you or judge you. I'm just trying to find the best fit for you in our system."

"Yes, Miss. I've never been in trouble. I worked hard. I kept to myself. I read and I worked. And I exercised. I never had time for anything else."

"All you did was work and read?"

"What else is there to do?" he asked.

She looked at him; she could see he was looking at her, too. She instinctively liked him. He was brave and strong. He was smart and not at all arrogant or crude. And, best of all, she could see that he was mentally disciplined, mentally tough. She admired this, and after their short talk, and observing his demeanor, it was her preliminary judgment that he probably was not a hard, conscienceless criminal. Her paramount consideration was to keep in mind that he had committed a hard core crime, and she would have to be very persuasive of her superiors to gain Americo entry into one of the pleasanter, lower security facilities. For this she needed more information, information she could only obtain from observing his reactions, as well as his answers, to questions concerning the choices and decisions he had made in his life.

Showing her radiant smile she leaned forward slightly, as if in confidence, and said, 'I think what you did was wrong, yet it was heroic, too."

Americo blushed. She noticed that, and was pleased.

"I did what I had to do. It was right. I know it was wrong, but it was right. He murdered my poppa. How could I live, knowing that he was alive and I did nothing?"

"How about telling the police?"

"I don't trust them. My poppa said not to trust them."

"Your poppa said not to trust anybody."

"He was right."

"You don't trust me?" She leaned forward a little closer. He could see some cleavage and he got very red. "I don't know. I'm not sure."

"We are going to get to know each other better, and I know you will trust me."

"How do you know?"

"Because I trust you."

His blood was pulsing quickly, and he felt the dizziness again.

"Let's go over your living arrangements before your father died."

"He didn't die. He was murdered."

"Before he was murdered. I don't like saying that."

"I don't like it, too, but that's what it is. It is disrespectful to make it nicer."

The woman looked at him, at his clear, direct gaze looking at her with intense focus, and she answered, "I agree with you. Now, please, tell me about your life before the murder."

"It was all very simple, plain." And he told her about the reading, the time boundaries, the library visits, the shoe-shine box and his trips to Forest Hills.

As he related this history she made notes, careful to get his words, which were important for his cause, better than the cold police-talk that the detectives used to notate the boy's dedicated, disciplined life, and his love of his father.

"I want to hear about the ordinary things that seem unimportant. Like your landlord and paying the rent."

"At the beginning of the month I would knock on his door and hand him the money."

"Who is he?"

"Mr. Inzerillo. He owns his house, and our home is attached to it."

"Our home?"

"Yes. My poppa and me."

She wrote in her book.

"Did Mr. Inzerillo speak to you? Did he ever ask any questions? About your father, or anything else."

"Yes. I would answer him. I would tell him my poppa couldn't walk so good, but that he says hello."

"And he never seemed suspicious."

"Never."

"And was it pretty much the same in the grocery store, and the other places?"

"It was the same. I did what I had to do, I bought this, I bought that, I paid, and said something pleasant, and that my father said hello."

"And you never felt that anyone was suspicious."

"No."

The woman looked at him for some moments.

"How about friends?"

"No. I wasn't sure I should know anybody too well. They would ask questions. My father taught me that. It would be dangerous."

"Your father taught you that."

"Yes." Then he added, "Except Annette."

"Annette?"

"A girl I met at the library."

"You like her?"

"Yes."

"Did you see her often?"

"Almost every week."

Did you spend time together? Did she come to your home?"

"No, nothing, we weren't really friends. I just liked her. We talked at the library."

"That was all?"

"She had no time. She worked at her father's newsstand in the city."

"So you never had a date with her."

Americo blushed. "I asked her to have lunch with me, but she couldn't. She wanted to. She liked me, too."

"What do you mean, too? You liked her and she liked you, too?"

"Oh, yes. I know that's true. We were so uncomfortable."

Miss Meskalik was a skilled interrogator, and she correctly saw the boy as having conflicting qualities not usually compatible. He had an attractive innocence and a scary wisdom. He had an unaffected charm while at the same time possessing a depth that could size things up clearly, giving him the ability to quickly grasp unfamiliar situations. And all the while there was in reserve a part of him that was ever watchful, and had proven to be capable of deadly cunning.

"What about Frankie?"

They talked about everything in the record that might raise a question for the hearing judge, probing the boy's mind, to get a good fix on who he was, and who he might become. He was so at ease in being forthcoming she was convinced he was being candid. She saw no signs of distortion or manipulation.

"You know, I wasn't looking for Luigi Leopardi. If I hadn't ever seen him I would never have done anything like this. I was invisible. Nobody knew anything about me. I didn't want to give that up."

"I can understand that."

"I liked my life."

"Weren't you lonely?"

"Yes."

"Yes."

"I was alone too much."

"You like talking with me?"

"Yes. But I don't want to be here."

"You've lost that choice."

"No. I didn't lose it. I gave it up. I did the right thing."

"I hope you learn to think otherwise."

"No. I know I will not."

As Miss Meskalik looked at him she was sadly thoughtful.

"I would never do anything like this again."

"No?"

"What would be the reason?"

"What if you thought you had a reason?"

Americo was surprised by this.

"That's why we have laws. And why you don't decide when it's right to break the law. You don't have that right. No one does." Her voice was becoming firmer.

"I know that," he spoke quickly, nearly interrupting her.

"Did you know it before?"

"Yes."

They sat quietly for some minutes, then she rose and indicated for him to get up. She walked to the door and waited for him, then opened the door. As he preceded her from the room she put a hand on his curly head and smiled her wonderful smile.

"You expected this? To be here?"

"Yes."

As they looked at each other the woman nodded her head, disappointed and sad.

CHAPTER TWENTY-FOUR

As THEY APPROACHED the desks where the detectives were sitting, Miss Meskalik said, "Here's your boy, Mac. We'll be ready for him at eleven, in the a.m. I'll be back for him."

"Call me. I'll bring him over."

With a negative nod she said, "No. I'll bring an attendant."

"See you in the a.m., he replied." And she left.

"Well, kid, I guess we're done here. I'll take you back to your cell. This'll be your last night in the cage."

"Enjoy it," said O'Halloran. "It'll be a long time before you're alone again."

They escorted him back to his cell. There was a new guard and as he selected the right key and unlocked the door O'Halloran and McGinnis said good-bye and walked away.

"May I have a cup of coffee?" Americo asked the guard.

New to his post, the guard, a husky, older patrolman,

many years on the job with no advancement, was irritated by the request and swung the back of his open hand against the side of the boy's head. The blow drove Americo to the floor, stunned and senseless.

"I'll be sending the maid in, later, sir," he hissed.

Americo lay on the floor a long while. Gradually he became aware that he was on the floor, and, in a half-conscious fog he crawled over to the bed and raised himself onto the mattress. It was chilly in the cell. He pulled the blanket over himself, and rested. As he lay there he fell into a light sleep. He had dreams of his life, as if his life was merely an accrual of episodes which he only experienced while sleeping. He saw his old home, with his father sitting in the armchair as they drank sweet tea together. Then he was sitting on a bench with Annette, laughing and eating sandwiches by the park pond. There was an infusion of happiness into his soul. Now he saw the librarian, with her bosom positioned by his face, and he felt warm, and snuggled in the blanket. Then there was Miss Meskalik, her smile distressing him as she put her hand in his hair, and he got warmer yet. Her hand in his hair felt delicious, and in his dream he wondered if he would always remember the excitement of her touch. He stirred, restless and groping in a dark place in which he suddenly saw his father, Giovanni, lying on the ground, with two men standing over him. One of the men moved toward him, into a patch of light. Luigi Leopardi, the murderer. And the other man, in the darkness, motioning. Who was that other man? Was that Frankie?

He was almost awake, now. He put his hand in his pocket to hold his father's ring, and in his sleep he heard his father sadly speak the inscription, "Amore, Philomena." He tried to remember his mother, but that memory was lost. He said the word, "Poppa," and fell asleep again, into a much deeper, dreamless sleep. He went from sleep into a coma, his breathing became difficult, and shortly before morning he died.

Two hours later the patrolman on the morning shift came on duty. Finding the boy, he immediately notified the captain who sent the two detectives hurrying to the cell. After taking in the sorry event McGinnis turned to the patrolman.

"What happened?"

"I don't know. That's how he was when I came in."

"Who was the duty patrolman during the night? What did he say when you got here?"

"Donohue? Nothing."

"You call the Medical Examiner?"

"He's coming right over."

He looked skeptically at the patrolman. "Go back to your desk."

The patrolman hesitated, nervous.

"Go on." McGinnis said in low voice, almost a whisper. "Go back to your desk. We'll take it from here."

With some sadness McGinnis looked at the body. Seeing the boy's hand in his pocket he gently drew it out. The fingers, in a loose fist, were holding the ring. In a gesture that could have been interpreted as showing sentiment he took the ring and put it in his pocket, next to his share of the boy's money.

O'Halloran wanted the odd two dollar bill, but he knew that wasn't going to happen.

CPSIA information can be obtained
at www.ICGtesting.com
Printed in the USA
LVHW032209260520
656626LV00002B/608